"I took down the wasp's nest from the porch this morning," Bryce said.

"You did?" Pleasure lit Sandi's face. Her smile sparkled genuine appreciation.

Oh, man, she was looking up at him like he was the king of the world. No ~~~~~ r her late husband, Keith, ~~~~~ nce. When she ~~~~~ und, she was pu ~~~~~ ur shirt button~~~~~

Bryce grinne~~~~~ ~~~~~ly basking in the momen~~~~~ as he secretly had last night when she'd come mighty close to flirting with him a time or two. Told him he was a handy man to have around. But why was he lapping up her praise like some kind of parched desert critter?

"Now you need to let me know if those wasps come back. They often try to rebuild a few times."

She nodded. "Okay."

"Promise?"

She nodded again.

They stood looking at each other, just like last night, her face lightly flushed.

Only, this time she wasn't mad at him.

Books by Glynna Kaye

Love Inspired

Dreaming of Home
Second Chance Courtship
At Home in His Heart

GLYNNA KAYE

treasures memories of growing up in small Midwestern towns—in Iowa, Missouri, Illinois—and vacations spent in another rural community with the Texan side of the family. She traces her love of storytelling to the many times a houseful of great-aunts and -uncles gathered with her grandma to share hours of what they called "windjammers"—candid, heartwarming, poignant and often humorous tales of their youth and young adulthood.

Glynna now lives in Arizona, and when she isn't writing she's gardening and enjoying photography and the great outdoors.

At Home in His Heart
Glynna Kaye

Love Inspired

Recycling programs
for this product may
not exist in your area.

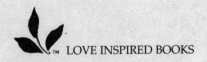 LOVE INSPIRED BOOKS

ISBN-13: 978-0-373-81568-5

AT HOME IN HIS HEART

Copyright © 2011 by Glynna Kaye Sirpless

www.LoveInspiredBooks.com

Printed in U.S.A.

Forget the former things; do not dwell on the past. See, I am doing a new thing! Now it springs up; do you not perceive it? I am making a way in the desert and streams in the wasteland.
— *Isaiah* 43:18–19

To my Aunt Betty, my "second mom,"
who is always in my corner and cheering me on—
and whose creativity, sense of humor, faith and
perseverance continue to inspire me.

Chapter One

Oh, man. Just his luck.

Sandi Bradshaw.

Keith's widow.

Bryce Harding stared down at the dainty blonde with shiny, blunt-cut hair, her long-lashed gaze leveled on him. Dark blue eyes reflected the same dismay that slugged him in the stomach when she'd turned toward him. She recovered faster than he did, though. Planting fists on her curvaceous, jeans-clad hips, she gave him a wary-eyed once-over, taking in his T-shirt, shorts and flip-flops.

"How may I help you—Sergeant?"

He forced cheerful warmth into his words. "I didn't know you worked here, Sandi."

Had he known, he'd have steered clear of Dix's Woodland Warehouse tonight. He liked to patronize locally owned businesses in his mountain-country hometown of Canyon Springs, Arizona. But a big-box store would have fit the bill just as well.

"I work here part-time when I'm not teaching school." She folded her arms, expression still guarded. "May I help you find something?"

"I—" Why was he scrambling for words just like he did last winter when he approached her? He'd voiced his sympathy concerning her loss. That seemed appropriate considering he and Keith had been buddies since second grade. But it had been an awkward meeting. She'd pretty much looked at him as if he'd sprouted antlers. Kind of how she was doing now. She'd murmured ill-at-ease words of thanks and that was that.

He'd tried to convince himself at the time it was because he'd caught her off-guard. Maybe she hadn't heard he'd gotten out of the army, had returned to town. But more likely, judging from the look on her face both then and now, her too-candid husband had spilled the beans. Told her about his best friend's campaign to keep him from marrying the cute little fox he'd fallen combat helmet over steel-toed boots for.

Sometimes, Bradshaw...

"I—" He cleared his throat and scrubbed the knuckles of one hand along the jawline of his beard. "I'm looking for one of those patch kits. You know, that putty you fix walls with."

"I'm afraid we don't carry anything like that." She sounded a little too pleased to share the news of a gap in the Warehouse's extensive inventory. "You'll need to go to the hardware store down the street."

"Already did. He's out of stock."

A perky eyebrow lifted. "If you've exhausted the local merchants, I'd say you're in for a drive to Pinetop-Lakeside's Home Depot."

She tilted her head, dipped her chin slightly and looked up at him—a mannerism that made his breath catch. A subtle bit of appealing body language that the way-too-smitten Keith had described to him in detail. More than once. Funny how he'd articulated it so well it seemed almost familiar now, not the mannerism of a stranger.

Pulling himself back to the conversation, he cleared his throat again. "Think I'll try the discount store first."

"You do that."

"I intend to."

He didn't need her approval to go to the discount store. To drive to Home Depot. To do anything. It appeared she'd changed little in the nine years since she'd first caught Keith's eye with that "Dear Soldier" letter of hers. Or since he himself had issued his buddy a disregarded warning. Keith laughed him off, but she was still a bit too pushy for his own tastes.

"Is there anything else you need?"

Obviously she wanted to get rid of him, but he wasn't going to let her shoo him out the door. Free country and all that.

"My grandma could use some…aspirin."

Though she had a medicine cabinet full of it.

Sandi's resolute expression transformed to one of concern. "Mae isn't feeling well?"

That's right, she knew his Grandma Harding. Grandma Mae he called her. "Arthritis is acting up."

She took an unexpected step forward, but his body blocked her and she pinned him with a pointed look. Guess she wanted him to get out of her way. After a moment's hesitation, he obediently stepped aside, the wooden floor creaking under his weight, but he caught the sweet scent of her as she maneuvered around him. Vanilla. Like Grandma Mae used in her chocolate chip cookies.

She motioned for him to accompany her as she headed down a store aisle. Past the souvenir items, sweatshirts and backpacks he followed along, determined not to let the alluring sway of her hips distract him.

After all, he was New Bryce now.

She was Keith's wife.

And not his type by a long shot.

She halted in front of a shelf and bent to snag an aspirin box. Placed it in his open palm. "This is what you want. Easier on the stomach, apparently."

He stared down at the box, then back at her. "You a nurse now or something?"

"No, but Sharon Dixon, who owns this store, is on an aspirin regimen for her heart. I've heard her talk about the benefits of this type." She pointed at the pain remedy. "Try this one."

"Does it come in a larger size?"

She took the box from his hand, her soft, slight one brushing his own, igniting his palm with a sensitivity he didn't know it possessed. Involuntarily his hand fisted, but a moment later she pried open his fingers to fill it with a supersize variety of the same aspirin brand.

"Anything else Mae could use? A heating pad, maybe? I've heard that sometimes helps."

He studied the cardboard container, then looked at her again. She sounded sincere enough. Helpful. Concerned about his grandma. Maybe this was the side of her she'd let Keith glimpse. Softening her—how should he put it?—uncompromising inclinations.

"I think this will do. Thanks."

"Very good." Her tone reverted to the impersonal, as if she'd again realized to whom she'd been talking—chatting with the man who'd done his best to save his buddy from a lifetime of regret. She headed back down the aisle. "I can check you out up at the front."

He followed her to the polished wooden counter and set the box down, then fished in a back pocket for his wallet. Pulled out a twenty, then broached a touchy subject. "I guess the museum will be open Memorial Day?"

With Sandi being the president of the local historical society, he'd had to call her several weeks ago. Had to notify her of upcoming changes to the agreement on the space his grandma leased to the Canyon Springs Historical Museum. It hadn't gone over well.

She gave him a probing glance as she rang up his purchase. "Is there a problem with the museum being open?"

"No. Just wondering what to expect."

"If you hadn't moved into the apartment above it with your grandma, you wouldn't be bothered by the historical society's comings and goings."

Grandma said Sandi had devoted herself to the museum since Keith's death, but who was she to judge if he should or shouldn't move in with his grandma? Grandma Mae was his first and only concern, and if her ability to remain relatively independent depended on having him close by, well so be it.

"Didn't say I was bothered. Just need to know what the plans are so I can keep my grandmother informed. After all, it is her home."

"I haven't forgotten that." Sandi's gaze sharpened as she handed him his change. His heart rate ramped up a notch, anticipating her fingers would again brush his, but she carefully placed the bills and coins into his palm without contact. "But it may have slipped *your* mind, Sergeant, that while you were dashing around the world on yet another tour of duty, the rest of us were right here making sure her needs were met."

No, maybe he hadn't been here, but nobody else managed to keep Grandma from falling down the back stairs, either. Or keep her from breaking her ankle, a wrist and a few ribs. He counted slowly to ten, determined not to let Keith's wife push his buttons. Grandma Mae always said the unspoken words you are master of, the spoken words are master of you.

Not that he'd always listened.

"That's something I'm well aware of, thank you, and for which I'm grateful."

"Then please make an effort to remember that—" her words came softly enough, but he didn't miss the underlying edge "—the next time you think about raising the rent on the historical museum and send us scrambling to make up the difference. That's why we're keeping it open on a holiday."

It was clear she thought the increase was nothing more than fun money for him. No doubt her husband had filled her in on the off-duty lifestyle of Old Bryce. Probably didn't know there was a New Bryce now. He hadn't exactly announced it to the town. She didn't know, either, that his volunteer work and part-time jobs were just biding time until the hiring freeze ended and that promised firefighter position opened up. Well, he wasn't going to explain his reasoning for the rent increase to her. It was nobody's business but his and Grandma Mae's.

Sandi tilted her head, her expressive eyes questioning, still waiting for a response to her pointed remark. But this time that cute little mannerism didn't stir him. Much. He shifted the gear of his tone into neutral and held up the aspirin box. "I'll keep your recommendation in mind. And thanks for your help."

He turned away and headed to the door, conscious of her annoyed stare piercing into his back.

A shame such a pretty little gal had a mile-wide unyielding streak. Nobody would ever guess looking at her—at the full, soft mouth, eyes the color of a twilight sky, the winsome little mannerisms.

A mighty big shame.

And he could see right now this museum business was going to put him in front of the firing line of her prickly disposition. Especially when she found out the museum's days were numbered.

But he'd keep that to himself for now.

"I have no intention of getting married again. Ever. And certainly not to *him*. So you can get that notion right out of your head, Devon." Sandi Bradshaw laughed at the look of dismay her words elicited from her pretty, matchmaking sister-in-law.

But at the mention of Bryce Harding's name her mind's eye had flashed to the big, dark-haired man with a neatly clipped beard and mustache who'd stood before her at the Warehouse last night. Twinkling brown eyes. Broad-shouldered and built like a bulldozer. If it weren't for the baggy cargo shorts, flip-flops and untucked black T-shirt emblazoned with No Regrets, she'd have thought he'd just stepped off the playing field of a Scottish highlands festival game.

But in the same instant she'd turned to him, his dark eyes had sobered with recognition and her own erratically pounding heart confirmed him as the man who'd come way too close to convincing her husband not to marry her.

"See?" Sandi's mother-in-law, LeAnne Bradshaw, shook back her stylishly cut, salt-and-pepper hair. She cast a knowing look at her daughter, Devon, across the glass-topped table of a Canyon Springs outdoor café—one of the many eateries and business establishments open only from Memorial Day weekend through Labor Day. "I told you Sandi and I are two of a kind. Each of us blessed beyond measure to have married the man of our dreams and no one else could ever replace either of them."

"I'm not saying anyone could replace Keith." Her expression still troubled as she eyed Sandi, Devon sliced off a bite of homemade apple pie. "But don't you remember, Sandi, how the two of you always laughed about wanting a house full of kids? Gina's already six years old. Don't you want any more children? Don't you ever get lonely?"

Remorse bayoneted Sandi's heart, her memory flashing to the last words she'd spoken to her husband. But she nevertheless rallied the same bright smile she determinedly affixed each morning. Tucking a strand of her chin-length hair behind an ear, she managed another little laugh. "I guess—"

"Oh, for goodness' sake, Devon, stop nagging the poor girl." LeAnne shot a withering look at her daughter. "When would she have time to get lonely? Teaching at the high school nine months out of the year. Church activities. And have you seen that 'to do' list of hers? Then there's Gina. She's more than a full-time handful."

"Well, all I can say—" Devon fixed Sandi with a playful look "—is if she's not fast on her feet, Sergeant

First Class Bryce Harding will be off the market in no time. I haven't been in town but a few hours and I'm already hearing he's the hottest item on this summer's menu."

Sandi's mind again rushed to the man who, prior to that first encounter last winter, she'd seen only in photographs. A man who'd had the nerve on that snowy day to stop her on the street, introduce himself and express his long-overdue condolences. She'd no idea he'd come back to town. Was so shocked at his unexpected introduction that she hadn't handled their meeting well.

At all.

Hadn't done so hot last night, either.

It had been no easy feat avoiding him since that first ill-fated encounter months ago. Not only did he escort his grandma to church on Sundays—looking as uncomfortable there as might be expected, given his lifestyle—but now he lived above the Canyon Springs Historical Museum. Right above her home away from home since Keith's untimely death five years ago.

With considerable effort, she directed a wink at her husband's little sister. "Help yourself to him, Dev. You'll have no competition from me."

No chance of that. Not in a million years.

With a sassy grin, Devon brushed a hand through her dark, shoulder-length hair and struck an alluring pose. "Maybe I will."

"Don't even think it." LeAnne tapped a well-manicured fingernail on the tabletop, a habit that set

Sandi's teeth on edge. Click. Click. Click. "You girls know how I feel about that man. Not someone I'd want either of you getting involved with. I don't care if he was Keith's friend."

Devon made a face. "Oh, Mom."

"He was obstinate and uncooperative as a kid and I doubt that's changed. A bad influence on Keith from the beginning. And his questionable reputation continues to precede him." LeAnne glanced around and lowered her voice to a whisper. "Besides, it's no secret his mother never married his father."

Sandi's sister-in-law smirked. "Like that's his fault?"

"He's too old for you, Devon." Click. Click. Click.

"He's Keith's age."

"Thirty-three to your twenty-three."

"I can do the math, Mom."

LeAnne turned to Sandi, putting a halt to her daughter's impertinence. "I suppose you'll be working the holiday weekend. But is it a good idea for Gina to spend so much time with that Diaz boy? All that tree climbing and rough-housing and—"

"Come on, Mom," her daughter cut in. "Now look who's nagging."

"I'm not nagging. I'm concerned."

"About what?" Devon wadded her napkin and tossed it on the table. "That the kid might be having *fun?*"

Sandi glanced at her watch and rose. Time to make her exit before these two got into it full-scale as they'd been known to do. She forced a lighthearted lilt into her voice. "Thank you for treating me to a birthday dinner. And on one of the nicest days weather-wise we've had this year. It's been fun."

She loved them both to pieces, but there was only so much Bradshaw fun she could take at a time.

"You're leaving already?" Devon wouldn't relish lingering alone with her mother.

As she'd done most of her married life, the now widowed elder Bradshaw retreated to the family's mountain home each year to escape the ovenlike temps of Phoenix—the Valley of the Sun. Devon, on the other hand, popped in on occasional weekends and only for as long as she and her mother could tolerate each other. It looked as if this might be an ultrashort weekend.

Sandi pulled her purse strap over her shoulder. "I'm filling in at the Warehouse a few hours this week. Kara Dixon's juggling the family business, working part-time with an affordable housing group and helping her fiancé at his High Country Equine Center. Grand opening's Memorial Day. Since Gina went to swimming lessons with a friend last evening and is at a sleepover tonight, I don't mind."

LeAnne sighed. "Is it necessary that you work at all in the summer, Sandi? Keith's daughter is at an age where she'll need a firm, guiding hand when school lets out next week."

Keith's daughter. She always threw that in there when she wanted to emphasize her daughter-in-law's mothering inadequacies.

She gave LeAnne a smile intended to reassure, not challenge, but explaining about the necessity for the job would ruin the surprise. Besides, it was already her intention to spend more time with Gina in the coming months. "I'll only be working part-time—afternoons several days a week—and Meg Diaz is as good of a mother stand-in as I could ever hope to find. Her stepson, Davy, is a wonderful little playmate for Gina, too."

"I'm not being critical, darling, it's just that—"

"Mom." Devon's voice again sliced into the conversation and the pair sat glaring at each other.

Definitely time to go.

Sandi bent to give each a speedy hug. They said their goodbyes with promises to get together soon, and with a sense of relief she headed down the street, drinking in the signature scent of Canyon Springs's ponderosa pine.

Although she and Keith's mother had settled into a fairly comfortable peace after his death, it was no secret her mother-in-law hadn't started out as her greatest fan. From the day Corporal Keith Bradshaw brought his bride home to meet the family, she hadn't pretended approval of the match.

After all, Sandi not only didn't hail from the country-club crowd, but had put herself through a less-than-prestigious Midwestern college on scholarships, student loans and minimum-wage jobs. To add to her unsuitable pedigree, her "introduction" to Keith came via a letter written in support of the troops while he was stationed in Iraq.

Not at all what Mommy envisioned for her youngest son.

As much as Sandi disliked the association, she and Bryce Harding had one thing in common: LeAnne Bradshaw's disdain of their dubious influence on her beloved baby boy. But in Bryce's case, her mother-in-law's perceptions were right on target.

A niggling unease swam up through the murky darkness of Sandi's subconscious. The same apprehension that assaulted her when she'd run into Bryce last winter. And again last night.

How much had her husband shared with him about their relationship? About her? About the quarrel that had haunted her for too many long, lonely nights in the wake of Keith's death?

And did she really want to know?

Chapter Two

"You're not real talkative tonight." Grandma Mae, her silver-gray hair tightly wrapped in pink plastic curlers, sat at the kitchen table across from him peeling potatoes into a pan nestled on her lap. Gnarled fingers clasped the handheld peeler Bryce had bought for her so she'd be less likely to cut herself with a knife. She wouldn't let him help with the chore. Said she had to keep her arthritic hands as limber as she could for as long as she could, and working with them was better than any medication she'd yet found.

She gave him a knowing look. "In fact, you're even less talkative than usual."

Bryce grunted as he turned to gaze out the window over the sink where the last dregs of sunlight filtered through the pine branches. God had been poking at him since yesterday. About Keith's wife. Wouldn't leave him alone. Saying he was being too hard on her. Needed to tell her about his plans for the museum, too. He'd seldom had to deal with that kind of prodding much B.J. Before Jesus. Keith would have said that was because he'd been like a kid with his eyes closed and his hands over his ears yelling *la la la la la*.

Sure was a lot of stuff he wished he could talk to Keith about now. Spiritual stuff. Women.

But it was too late.

He turned back to the woman who'd raised him, who knew him better than anybody else did. "Nothing much to say, I guess."

She fixed him with a scrutinizing eye. "Are you regretting coming back here?"

"No."

"Awfully small town for such a big man." She set the pan on the table, pushed both it and a cutting board toward him to indicate he could do the slicing. Then she grasped the arm of the chair as she attempted to pull herself to her feet. Bryce was halfway out of his own chair to assist her, but she waved him off and accomplished it on her own. Shuffled to the sink, still favoring that ankle she'd broken late last fall. "Not a whole lot exciting going on around here for someone who's lived off an adrenaline rush for fifteen years."

"Overrated." He placed a potato on the cutting board and reached for a wooden-handled knife. He'd had enough of that kind of excitement to last him a good long while. Iraq. Afghanistan. Bad enough he dreamed about it. Woke up in a cold sweat.

In comparison, firefighting in a tiny town would seem like child's play. Not that he'd mention that to the fire chief who'd promised to back his application. But nobody in Canyon Springs—you'd hope anyway— would be waiting in ambush when you raced in to put out a fire.

Grandma turned on the faucet. "Don't imagine there's much around here in the way of young single women, either."

Sandi Bradshaw's wide-eyed gaze flashed through his mind. He took aim with the knife and gave the potato a whack. A chunk flew into the air and landed on the worn linoleum floor. He bent to pick it up. "That's overrated, too."

She snorted, and he couldn't suppress a grin.

He'd never confided to her the details of his life in the military, but undoubtedly she'd filled in the blanks on her own, wise woman that she was. No point in denying it. He'd sowed his share of wild oats.

And then some.

Wasn't proud of it. But what was done was done and now in the past.

He changed the subject. "Do you want to go to the Memorial Day parade on Monday? I'd be happy to take you."

He didn't much care for parades himself, but he'd dress like a clown and stand on his head in the middle of it if that would make Grandma Mae happy.

"I'd like that."

"Then it's a plan. So, Gran, what'd you do today?" He sliced another potato—with less gusto this time.

"Peggy came by and set my hair." She patted her

curlers. "Then I watched a little TV. Did some reading."

He had reading to do, too, if what was in the box sitting on his bed was what he thought it was. Grandma had been at him to join the men's summer group at Canyon Springs Christian Church. But he'd taken one look at the syllabi posted in the fellowship hall a few Sundays ago and decided it wasn't for him.

Not that he couldn't use some help in the God department, but a big chunk of it focused on how to be the head of a household. A husband. A parent. He'd feel out of place among all those married guys. Dads. Grandpas. He didn't put much stock in what others thought about him, good or bad. But this was different. He'd look downright silly to them. Green as grass.

It was stuff he needed to know, though, if he was going to be the kind of man he should have become a long time ago. All the stuff Keith kept telling him—and he hadn't listened. Blew him off. But going to the men's study would be like a rookie recruit marching out with a bunch of battle-hardened, heavily equipped veterans—without guns and gear. In skivvies even.

There was nothing to stop him, though, from ordering online the CDs and workbook they were using. So that's what he'd done. Ordered a volume on Arizona history, too, just in case Grandma asked what was in the box.

Yeah, he had a lot of catching up to do. But he

didn't want to think about why, since his encounter with Sandi yesterday, that it seemed more urgent than before.

Sandi would give just about anything not to have to make this call.

But all too often doing the dirty work was synonymous to her role as the president of the historical society. Right now calling Bryce Harding fell into that category. Why'd the electricity have to go out tonight? Just when she'd slipped in to catch up on work? But with the museum set to be open Saturday and Monday, she didn't dare hope the situation would resolve itself. Since Mae's grandson seemed to be sticking his nose in museum business now, she'd let him deal with it.

She speed-dialed Mae's number on her cell phone. Had the power gone out upstairs, too? She glanced around the darkened room of the old stone house which sat a block off Main Street, surrounded by trees. At nine o'clock and with leafed-out bushes and bristly pines snuggled in close, hardly any light came in from the street. She gave an involuntary shudder.

It was creepy here at night.

In the dark.

Alone.

"Hello?"

Startled when the phone picked up on the first ring and a familiar masculine voice responded, she steadied herself by launching in with her most businesslike tone. "This is Sandi Bradshaw. I'm downstairs at the museum. The power is out, although it looks like the neighbors still have lights. Do you?"

"Yeah. You probably blew a fuse down there."

She waited expectantly, but he didn't offer a solution.

"Is that something you can do something about? I have work to do here tonight and the museum will be open tomorrow."

He paused as if debating her request, then it seemed he'd covered the mouthpiece with his hand for she could hear indistinguishable words in his rumbling voice. Probably consulting with Mae. When he returned he seemed to speak with reluctance. "Grandma has extra fuses. Hang on."

The phone went dead.

She crammed it back into her purse. No wonder he'd long infuriated LeAnne, why she was so adamant about daughter and daughter-in-law giving him wide berth. How had her charming husband gotten along so well with him since childhood? She had no choice, though, but to wait for Bryce to ride to the rescue.

When at last she heard him on the porch at the rear of the house, she stubbed a sandaled toe on a chair as she made her way through the outdated kitchen that the historical society still used on occasion. By the time she got to the door, he'd already used his key and let himself in.

He had a flashlight, one of those sturdy man-type ones that could sit on the floor and direct a beam with a tilt-type head. It illuminated the room, throwing a massive shadow of his broad-shouldered body to the wall behind him.

"Thanks for coming."

He nodded, then moved past her. Shining the light around the room, he flipped a wall switch. The room remained dark.

She refrained from a smug I-told-you-so.

He wordlessly glanced in her direction as if reading her mind, then maneuvered around the table and headed to the front of the house. She followed, relieved to have another human being in the darkened building even if that person had to be Bryce. Didn't hurt either that he looked as if he could take on anything that might spring out of the shadows at them.

He halted and turned, looking surprised to see her tailgating so closely. "What are you working on that can't wait until tomorrow?"

Meaning, why did he have to get out of his cushy recliner and surrender the TV remote to Grandma so he could do this right this very minute?

"I'm inventorying a donation of photographs that came in this week. Early days of Canyon Springs. Perfect timing since my daughter is celebrating a birthday with friends tonight."

His brow wrinkled. "But it's not her birthday, right? That's in April."

He remembered that?

"Right."

He nodded at her confirmation and moved into the main room of the museum. Flipped another switch.

Got a clue now, Sergeant?

Maneuvering around her, he headed back through the kitchen to an adjacent room that once served as a pantry. Now it housed a hodgepodge of boxes containing the town's memorabilia and office supplies. She stood in the doorway, acutely aware of the diminutive dimensions of the space as he set the flashlight on a shelf. Then with a long-suffering look in her direction, Bryce lifted down from the wall a gingham-decorated bulletin board to reveal a metal panel. Fuse box. What did he expect? She couldn't leave that ugly gray thing protruding like that.

She returned to the front room to allow him to do whatever he needed to do in peace. Rummaging through her purse with a lighted key chain, she found the red, spiral notebook that contained her checklist. Perfect. If he intended to raise the rent, she may as well negotiate more bang for the buck.

A few minutes later, blinding light flooded the room from the overhead fixture. While her eyes were still adjusting to the abrupt contrast, he joined her.

"Wow. Thanks. You're a pretty handy guy to have around."

Now why'd she say something stupid like that? Sounded almost like flirting. She didn't flirt. Hadn't since Keith. Wasn't going to start now.

Bryce gave her an assessing look. "It appears you're back in business."

"So it was a blown fuse? What would cause that? I didn't have a bunch of appliances on at the same time."

He shrugged. "No telling. Maybe a power surge. Decrepit fuse."

"Well, thanks. And while you're here—" She flipped through the pages of her pocket-size notebook. "Would you mind taking a look at a few other maintenance-related things?"

From the pained expression that clouded his eyes, it looked as though his TV remote must be calling his name.

"They wouldn't have to be done right this minute," she hurried on. "But if I could point them out now, then you could take care of them later. Not as in a hundred years from now, but later."

"Like what?"

She ran her finger down the list. "The toilet runs excessively. Wastes water. We have to remember to jiggle the handle to get it to stop. Wasps built a nest on the porch, above the front door. Not good. And the outlet in the kitchen where we plug in the coffeemaker is dead."

She motioned him to follow her to the front room where she demonstrated a creaking floorboard. "Obnoxious, isn't it? And there's a crack in the window of the bedroom we use for storage, the miniblinds on the front window are stuck half-opened and the dead bolt on the back door is almost impossible to latch."

"That all?"

"Oh, and the kitchen faucet drips." She glanced again at her list. "Several other things, but they can wait."

"Who took care of this stuff for you this time last year?"

"What?"

"Who did your maintenance work before I came back to town?"

"Well, I have the past few years." She stuffed the notebook back in her purse. "Or at least I've done what I could or hired someone to do it."

He raised a brow, his expression mildly amused as he studied her. "And now suddenly—?"

Her face warmed. Was he intimating that she'd abdicated her responsibilities so she could coerce him into spending time with her?

"You're raising the rent. It seems only right that more property upkeep should be included. With every passing year more things go wrong, more expensive things. Like the window air-conditioning unit last summer. Tearing out and upgrading the sidewalk so no one would trip and sue us. Roof repair. Replacing the furnace which also, incidentally, heats the upstairs."

He looked round the room, all evidence of previous amusement vanished. "Maybe it's time the society found a more adequate facility. This is an old house. Old plumbing, old wiring, old roof. Maintenance comes with the territory."

"I understand that." How dare he suggest they vacate the premises because she was asking for reasonable accommodation? "But I also understand from Meg and Kara who worked with you on the parsonage remodel that you're quite capable at that type of repair work. You could do it at a fraction of the cost it would be for us to hire someone."

He was silent a long moment, as if weighing the value of her requests. Was he thinking he owed her husband to help out his widow? Or that as luck would have it, a premature passing had saved his buddy a lifetime of heartache? She hated not knowing how much he knew about her and Keith.

At long last he nodded. "I'll see what I can do."

He was agreeing? Without further argument? If he was in such a willing mood, maybe she should have read the whole list to him. Who knew when there might be another opportunity like this?

"Thank you," she managed, deflated that the need to defend the historical society's rights had evaporated so easily.

"You're welcome." He took a few steps toward the kitchen, then paused to look at the crowded display cases and antique furniture. At the framed photographs, maps and documents lining the walls. Then he did an appraising once-over of *her*. A look that left her, of all the ridiculous things, wishing she'd combed her hair before leaving the Warehouse. Applied a little lipstick.

What was her problem tonight?

"Don't take this the wrong way." He gave the room another sweeping glance, then focused dark, considering eyes on her. "But you need to get a life."

What?

She huffed a laugh of disbelief. "Excuse me?"

"I told you not to take it wrong."

"And how could I take a comment like that right?"

He shrugged and moved again toward the kitchen with her hot on his heels. "Don't you think common courtesy demands you elaborate after saying something as judgmental as that?"

He halted in the arched doorway between the two rooms and again turned, his gaze solemn. "I think you know what I'm talking about."

"Now I'm a mind reader?"

He waved a hand, indicating the museum as a whole. "Grandma says you and Gina have practically lived at this place. I know I see your car here frequently."

"So?"

"So, do you think Keith would have wanted you to seal yourself up in this tomb? Digging through musty old stuff that belonged to dead people?"

With a gasp, her gaze flew to the photograph of her husband on the wall, his medals in the frame beside it. Hands on her hips, she stepped to within inches of Bryce. "I happen to appreciate history—and love some of those dead people."

He didn't so much as flinch. Just stared down into her eyes, some elusive emotion she couldn't pinpoint flickering through his own.

Mesmerized, her heart rate quickened. She shouldn't have moved in so close. To where she could feel the heat emanating from him. See the rising and falling of his chest. The pulse at his throat. Smell a faint, shower-fresh masculine scent.

With an abrupt movement, he broke eye contact and stepped back. "I'm sorry. I wasn't referring to Keith. My apologies."

Then he swung around and headed to the back door.

For a moment she almost followed him. Almost let him have a piece of her mind. But what good would that do? His poking his nose into her business had started when she'd first met Keith—and it didn't appear to have let up. Chasing after him now would only hand him another opportunity to voice judgment on her personal life.

A place where his observations weren't welcome.

Chapter Three

"That man infuriates me, Meg. He's just so, so—"

"Buff?" Her high school teaching colleague laughed as she refilled their glasses with icy, home-made lemonade. Sandi had stopped by after work late Saturday afternoon to pick up Gina.

Memory rushed against her will to the imposing, well-built man. Solid as a rock. "Very funny. I'm thinking more along the lines of mulish and interfering."

"Are you kidding me?" Meg's eyes widened as she placed the pitcher on the kitchen table and sat down across from her. "Are we talking about the same man? The Bryce Harding I know is a big lovable, huggable bear of a guy."

"How would you feel about your Mr. Buff if he'd tried to stop your husband from marrying *you?* He had it in his head I was going to ruin Keith's life. Even emailed him from overseas on our wedding day. Can you believe it? Keith showed it to me at the reception. Thought it was funny."

"What did it say?"

"Last chance, bud. Bus departs at two."

Meg let out a gleeful yelp, then clapped her hand momentarily to her mouth. "Sorry. But Sandi, that's no big deal. That's how guys talk to each other. They can't express their feelings well. Half the time they can't even identify for themselves what they're feeling. That was just Bryce's way of saying 'hey, dude, gonna miss ya.'"

"I'm afraid there's more to it than that."

"Hey, don't you remember?" Meg's eyes continued to dance. "At my wedding reception, right before we cut the cake, one of Joe's old navy buddies snuck up and clamped a fake ball and chain around my hubby's ankle. That's just guys."

"I remember. But this is different. Way different."

"You're blowing a joke out of proportion, Sandi. Seriously. Bryce is one of the good guys."

"You wouldn't think that if you knew about him what I know about him."

"Maybe the man you knew has changed. Joe said Bryce quit going to church with his grandma when he was in high school. But he goes now. Doesn't that count for anything?"

She couldn't tell Meg how Keith had worried about Bryce. About his wild ways. His hard drinking and hard partying. His superficial relationships with women. Keith had done his best to influence Bryce, to convince him he wasn't really living unless he was living for God. But Bryce the Bullheaded carried on in the direction he was determined to go—and good-naturedly badgered Keith to join him on his journey.

"As the old saying goes, Meg, sitting in a garage doesn't make you a car."

"It's a start."

"Maybe." Guilt nibbled around the edges of her conscience. She'd been kind of snippy with him at the Warehouse and again at the museum last night. Not that he didn't deserve it, but that wasn't how Keith—or God—would want her treating him. "Because of his interference, Keith delayed proposing. We could have been married who knows how much earlier if Bryce hadn't poked his nose in where it didn't belong. That's time Keith and I'll never get back."

Time that maybe she could have grown up more. Done things differently.

"But if you'd have married earlier," Meg said, her gaze steady, "even if you got pregnant right away like you did with Gina, your baby wouldn't have *been* Gina."

"I know." Sandi toyed with the ribbon on a basket of spa-type goodies that Meg had given her for her birthday. "And I wouldn't trade her for the world."

She glanced out the open French doors to the patio, where Meg had several flats of petunias awaiting transplant. Could smell the sweet fragrance. Hear the laughter of their precious children coming from some-where under the long-shadowed pines.

"But can't you see why I'm not thrilled about Bryce's homecoming?" She poked at an ice cube with the tip of her finger. "I hear he's doing odd jobs. Not what I'd call earning-a-living work. Moved in with his grandma—like she needs *him* to deal with. And now he's announced the historical museum rent will go up when the lease renews."

Meg cringed. "You're on a tight budget, aren't you?"

"Even with measly city assistance we're barely hanging on, what with the drop in seasonal visitors. And of course Bryce raises the rent right when I've almost saved enough money to donate a display case. Right when I'm prepared to approach the board about expanding our miniscule armed services exhibit to a room of its own. But unless summer revenues rebound or we can drum up more local support, that won't happen anytime soon—thanks to Sergeant Harding."

"Maybe he didn't have a choice. Mae could need the money."

"More likely *he* does." Wine, women and song didn't come cheap.

Meg sipped at her lemonade, struggling to suppress a smile.

"What?"

"Oh, I just seem to recall that less than a year ago I, too, met a certain single someone over a bottle of aspirin at Dix's Woodland Warehouse." She waved a hand around the kitchen of their newlywed home. "And look where I am today."

Sandi wagged a warning finger. "Don't even—"

"Mommy! Mommy!" two giggling, childish voices yelled in unison. The screen door off the laundry room slammed behind them, then her almost-first-grade daughter and classmate pal Davy Diaz charged into the kitchen. Davy threw himself into his mother's open arms just as Gina did likewise with her own mom. Hugs all around.

"Oh, my goodness." Meg brushed back her stepson's black hair to reveal a smudged forehead that matched his grimy cheeks. "How'd you two get so dirty?"

"We're building Gilligan's Island," Davy managed to get out, still attempting to catch his breath. "On that big pile of dirt Daddy dumped back there. I'm Gilligan and Gina's Skipper."

"Can you believe it, Meg? *Gilligan's Island* fans. Third generation. Thank goodness for DVDs." Sandi allowed Gina to climb onto her lap. Then, slipping her arms around her daughter's waist, she smiled down at the pigtailed tomboy who, except for the blond hair and freckles, looked so much like her daddy. "Let's get you home and cleaned up."

Gina's shoulders slumped. "I like being dirty."

"I know you do. But tomorrow's a church day."

Gina pointed at her playmate. "You goin', Davy?"

He nodded his head in exaggerated agreement. "Yup."

Sandi gathered up their things, then Meg and Davy escorted them to their car.

"Thanks for agreeing to take care of Gina a few afternoons a week this summer, Meg. I can't tell you how much I appreciate knowing she'll have a safe and happy place to go. The afterschool babysitter this year has been cranky and impatient. Not good with kids at all."

"You know I'm more than happy to have her here. She and Davy get along so well. Seldom fight."

"Thank goodness." She turned to the driver's door, but Meg's hand stayed her, eyes troubled.

"I know I don't know everything there is to know about him like you do, Sandi, but I think you're wrong about Bryce."

"Don't I wish." She gave her friend a halfhearted smile.

But she wouldn't hold her breath.

"Hey, big fella."

Bryce felt a nudge and looked up from the Warehouse shelves where, crouched and arms full, he'd been gathering items for museum-repair jobs.

"Hey, Kara." He rose to his feet, taking in the tall, ponytailed woman beside him, her red-blond hair shimmering down her back. "How are things in your world?"

"Good. Grand opening of the equine center's almost here. Thanks for giving Trey a hand." She motioned to the merchandise cradled in his arms. "How about you? Looks like you're planning serious home repair."

"Not quite, but close. Canyon Springs Historical Museum."

Kara laughed. A laugh he well remembered from when she'd helped him when he'd filled in for another guy on the parsonage remodel last winter. A Canyon Springs hometown girl who'd spent time as a Chicago interior designer, she'd been a much-needed ally at making the place female friendly without going overboard on foo-foo stuff as some of the church ladies had pushed for.

"Didn't take long for Sandi to put you to work, did it?" Kara folded her arms, eyes bright with amusement. "I'm told that 'to do' list of hers keeps half this town hopping."

"So I'm not its only victim?"

"No, but from looking at what you have there, I'm guessing you got more than your fair share."

"That's what I thought." He shook his head, not quite understanding how he let her push the projects off on him. He should have stood his ground. Backed her down when she started in with that "it seems only right" stuff. Not let her manipulate him the way she'd done poor old Keith.

She'd made it no secret back then that she wanted her husband out of the service—and out of Canyon Springs. Grandma said she still lived in that house trailer Keith bought at the end of his third year in the service, back when he dreamed of spending hard-earned leave time in the mountains fishing from dawn until dusk. Bryce always figured Keith's bride would vacate right after his buddy was settled six feet under.

So what was she still doing here?

Kara glanced toward the Warehouse entrance, her

smile widening. "Looks like someone's checking up on you, Sergeant."

He followed her gaze to the door, where Sandi had just entered, looking mighty pretty in a pair of below-the-knee shorts and blue knit top. Proceeding to the back of the store, she didn't look his way. Hadn't seen him. He could sneak out. Come back later. He couldn't let her think she had only to snap her fingers and he'd come running. He should have put the supply trip off a few days. Weeks. Made her wait.

"Would you mind holding this stuff for me up front, Kara?"

"Be happy to."

He walked with her to the checkout counter, where she had him place his items off to the side. "I'll be back shortly."

Almost to the door he halted. He'd likely see Sandi at church tomorrow, wouldn't he? Did he want her dogging him about the repairs in front of other people? Maybe he should let her know he was on top of things. Didn't need a drill sergeant to keep tabs on him. Remind her he was his own boss, set his own timelines.

He headed toward the back of the store with determined steps. Rounding the corner in front of a towering paper towel display, he almost collided with Sandi. In one arm she cradled two cereal boxes, a bag of bagels and a loaf of bread. Her other hand clutched a gallon milk jug.

Startled, she stepped back, directing a frown at him.

"Sorry, Sandi. Let me help you with that."

With some reluctance—or so it seemed to him—she relinquished the armload. She was probably still mad that he'd told her she needed to get a life. It was the truth, but maybe he shouldn't have been so brusque. Then again, if *she* could be bossy, why couldn't *he* be blunt?

"Thanks." She gripped the milk jug tightly, an uncertain gaze flitting to his.

He gave the grocery items a once-over. "Looks like breakfast."

She ran a hand through her silky hair. "It dawned on me as Gina and I were heading home that I didn't have a single breakfast item in the house."

He glanced around but didn't see the kid.

"She's outside talking to a friend," Sandi said, correctly interpreting the question in his eyes. She snagged a jar of peanut butter off a nearby shelf. "So are you still looking for a patch kit?"

"Actually—" Should he grab a bottle of orange juice and a carton of eggs to camouflage his intent? Naw. "I'm picking up stuff for museum repairs. Hitting the hardware store next."

Although filled with disbelief, her eyes brightened. "Wow. Thank you. I didn't expect you'd get to it quite this fast."

"Is that a problem?"

"No, no. Not at all. Marking things off my checklist is never a problem."

"I'm booked for the rest of the weekend assisting Trey at the equine center, so the repairs won't happen overnight."

"I understand. Totally."

"Didn't want your checklist waiting with bated breath—although I did take down the wasp's nest first thing this morning."

"You did?" Pleasure lit her face as she did that cute little head-tilt thing. Her smile sparkled with genuine appreciation.

Oh, man, she was looking up at him as if he was the king of the world. No wonder poor old Keith hadn't stood a chance. When she wasn't busy bossing you around, she was pumping up your ego until your shirt buttons popped off.

He grinned down at her, openly basking in the moment—just as he secretly had last night when she'd come mighty close to flirting with him a time or two. Told him he was a handy man to have around. But why was he lapping up her praise like some kind of parched desert critter? It wasn't as if he'd never gotten attention from an attractive woman before.

Been plenty of those.

What made this any different?

He sobered, not sure he wanted an answer to that question. "Now you need to let me know if those wasps come back. They often try to rebuild a few times."

She nodded. "Okay."

"Just let me know."

"All right."

"Promise?"

She nodded again.

They stood looking at each other, just like last night when she'd marched up to him and demanded an explanation for his insensitive comment about musty rooms and dead people's belongings.

Only this time she wasn't mad at him.

But she would be if she knew what he was thinking. Old Bryce for sure. He cleared his throat and shifted the groceries in his arms. "Let me take this stuff up front for you."

"Thanks. I need to get Gina home and fed."

He followed her, resolutely keeping his gaze focused anywhere but on Sandi. Only a couple of days and he was already starting to think stupidly. Act stupidly. Probably had a goofy look on his face, too.

Just like the one Keith had.

But she was a woman no sane man would take more than a passing glance at if he had a mind of his own. Didn't want to be ordered around like some wet-be-hind-the-ears army recruit for the rest of his life.

It looked as if he'd better do his museum repairs during closing hours—when Sandi was off the premises.

Chapter Four

"Mommy, tell me about the time Daddy took me to see the guinea pigs at the pet shop."

Sandi pulled her thoughts from the latest encounter with Bryce Harding—he'd already taken down the wasp nest—and wrapped her dripping-wet daughter in a big fluffy towel.

"I'll tell you about the guinea pigs while we eat supper, okay?"

Gina had been asking for daddy stories ever since they'd left Meg's. Apparently Davy's tales of all the things he and his father had done since Joe's return from the navy last year had sparked her own need for a renewed connection to the man she didn't remember. She'd already been told the guinea pig story on the way home, but now she demanded it again. When you were only a year old when your daddy died, there weren't that many stories to choose from.

A heaviness settled into Sandi's chest as she finished drying Gina and got her into her pajamas. It was still daylight, but with the fresh air and hard play it was evident Gina would be ready for bed soon after they ate. And sure enough, a small bowl of soup and half a sandwich later she couldn't keep her eyes open. Tucked into bed at Bradshaws-in-the-Pines—as Keith had dubbed their house trailer in keeping with local custom—Gina was asleep the moment her head hit the pillow.

No more daddy stories tonight.

Busy days ahead, though, so tomorrow after church they'd both rest. Monday was Memorial Day and, except for her two-hour afternoon slot at the museum, she'd promised the whole day to Gina. Parade. Petting zoo. Face painting. The works.

Just as she pulled her daughter's bedroom door closed, her cell phone rang and she hurried to the kitchen, where she'd left it on the counter.

"Hi, doll," a warm female voice greeted her. "Happy belated birthday."

"Thanks, Sharon." Envisioning her friend Kara's mother, owner of Dix's Woodland Warehouse, she flipped off the glaring overhead kitchen light then strolled into the shadowed living area of the open floor-planned space.

"How'd things go for your birthday dinner last night?"

"Pretty good. Devon was there, so that helped. Thanks for the prayers." She sat down on the sofa and stretched out socked feet to rest on the coffee table.

"It's always hard when LeAnne first comes back for the summer, but after a few weeks it will be okay."

"I know you've grown closer through the years."

"I think the world of her. But I wish I wouldn't always remember how she never wanted Keith to marry me in the first place. I still can't seem to shake that."

Nor could she shake off the certainty that her mother-in-law had been right. She hadn't deserved Keith. Wasn't worthy of him. But she'd never spoken aloud that conviction—and why she believed it—to anyone. Ever.

"Now stop that right now. It doesn't matter what Keith's mom did or didn't want. What's important is what Keith wanted. And he wanted to spend the rest of his life with you."

"Guess he did that all right, huh?" She gripped the phone tighter. "The remaining two years of it anyway."

Had she only known Keith four years—and most of that long distance? And only been married to him barely two of those?

"Doll, am I going to have to come over there tonight and—"

"No, no." Sandi laughed, picturing Sharon clomping into the room on her walker to pull her into a big bear hug and give her a good chewing out. "I'm not going to lower myself into a pity-party pit. I promise."

"Good. Now get yourself into a bubble bath with a good book. The opening hurdle with your mother-in-law is behind you."

But what about the hurdle that yet faced her with Bryce Harding back in town? She'd managed to avoid him until now, done her best to forget he even existed. But Thursday night's inevitable encounter—and two subsequent ones—brought home that even though he hadn't uttered a word about it, he still thought she'd been all wrong for Keith.

She hated his being right.

The two friends said their goodbyes, but when Sandi shut off the phone it immediately rang again. It was LeAnne Bradshaw. For a too-tempting moment she almost let it go to messaging.

"Sandi, I just found out the club is bringing in a San Francisco pianist for brunch tomorrow morning. I've heard he's divine. You and Gina must join Devon and me."

Must?

Golf, tennis, bridge and book-club chats filled her mother-in-law's days behind the walls of the gated community where she resided three months out of the year. Nevertheless, Sandi long ago recognized Keith's mom was lonely.

Like her.

If the pianist played early enough, maybe they could still get back in time for their morning's commitments. "When will—"

"Ten o'clock. Nothing fancy. A sundress is fine."

"Church starts at ten-thirty." LeAnne must have forgotten.

"You go to church every week, don't you?" Her mother-in-law sounded puzzled, as if not understanding her hesitation. "It's not every day a concert pianist of Philemonn's caliber comes to the high country. Gina needs to be exposed to some of the finer things that small towns don't usually provide."

"I know, but we—"

"I'm not taking no for an answer this time, Sandi. You need to treat yourself and Gina to something special every so often. I realize you didn't have these opportunities growing up like Keith did. But he'd want that for you. For Gina."

"Maybe we—" They could go to the early church service.

"Good. Then it's settled. And while we're lunching, let's plan our Memorial Day visit to the cemetery."

She took a steadying breath. "I went early this morning. Took Gina."

"You did?" The affront in LeAnne's voice came through clearly—*without me?*

In the past they'd gone together. But for some reason Sandi couldn't put into words, she'd needed to go alone this year. With her daughter.

"It just worked out better for me with my work schedule and museum obligations."

"I see." Unspoken words of hurt and reprimand hung in the air.

Although she couldn't hear them over the phone, LeAnne's well-manicured nails would certainly be clicking away, counting the seconds until Sandi came up with an alternative proposal. She didn't want to go again. Summer hadn't even started yet and time alone with Gina already seemed to be slipping away. But LeAnne was Keith's mom, whom he'd loved dearly and worried about after his father's death. Accompanying her to the cemetery was the least she could do, if for no other reason than the most glaring one—she owed it to Keith.

"Maybe we could go Sunday afternoon?" she offered, capitulating. "After the brunch?"

There was a long silence, as if LeAnne was deciding whether to accept the offer graciously or refuse and leave her daughter-in-law to repay her in some other way at a later time.

"I don't want to disrupt your schedule. But you know it is a family time, a time to remember and honor Keith."

Did she think Sandi didn't remember Keith daily? Wasn't doing her best to honor him?

When she didn't respond, LeAnne continued. "So that's what we'll do. And tomorrow we'll plan our Friday nights for the remainder of the summer, as well. Maybe a movie this week if we can find something suitable for Gina. Oops. Have to go. Another call coming through. See you tomorrow."

Sandi shut off the phone and leaned back into the sofa. She sat in the fading twilight for a seemingly endless stretch of time, staring across the room to where she knew a framed photo of Keith rested on a built-in bookcase shelf. If only…

How many things she would change if only she could.

A few words. Spiteful, wounding words she couldn't take back. Words that drew an immovable line in the sand. Words—born of fear for Keith's safety and her own loneliness—that demanded that if he didn't quit the military, didn't come home immediately, she'd have no more children with him.

The flash of headlights from a vehicle traveling along the hard-packed gravel-and-dirt road momentarily illuminated the photograph. The proud smile and twinkling eyes of her husband seemed to focus on her as he cradled Gina on his lap.

Her first birthday.

Three months later he was gone.

And yesterday was her own birthday. Twelve months from now she'd hit the Big Three-Oh. If she lived the life expectancy of an average American woman, that left another fifty years.

Without Keith.

Alone.

Sandi sank deeper into the sofa as the car with the headlights passed by and the room returned to darkness.

"Move!"

Something shoved roughly against Bryce's leg as the high school band down the street struck up the opening bars of the "Star-Spangled Banner." Almost caught him off-balance as he'd leaned over to speak to his grandma, seated in the wheelchair next to him.

What the—? He shifted, glancing down to see the ball-capped head of a kid pulling back to give him another hearty shove. He grabbed one of the hands. "Hey. Cut that out, kid."

The child jerked free, head tilting up to look at him. Chin jutting and eyes flashing.

Bryce chuckled. A girl. And except for the affronted expression, she was the spittin' image of her daddy. He turned to scan the faces around him, expecting to see her mother nearby. No sign of her. But he couldn't be mistaken about this kid's identity. The resemblance to her father was striking, and he'd caught occasional glimpses of her at church, too.

He squatted to eye level. "What's the problem here?"

"I can't see." She pushed back the oversize ball cap—desert camouflage with an army insignia—and put her hands on her hips in a gesture that reminded him of her mom. "You're too big. You hafta move."

If he hadn't any other clue as to her maternal parentage, that sealed the deal. Only another Bradshaw female would tell him what to do. Without a second thought, he handed his Western hat to his grandma. Then he lifted the now-giggling child over his head to sit atop his shoulders, her jeans-clad legs horseshoe-ing around his neck.

He grasped her ankles to steady her. "How's that, little lady? Can you see now?"

She giggled again, tiny hands pressing against his forehead as she tilted it back to look into his face. "Do I know you?"

"I'm a friend of your daddy." Should have said mom, too, but that would be stretching it.

"You know my daddy?"

"I sure do." Did. "We were like brothers."

"Mommy!" She released him and he felt her twisting and turning, searching in vain for her parent. "Mommy! Guess what?"

He patted her leg. "Hey, hey. Pipe down. The band's coming."

A moment later the color guard with the Stars and Stripes of the United States of America passed by. Bryce's heart swelled as his hand shot up in salute, and he caught the eye of his friend Joe Diaz across the way likewise standing at attention.

The little girl leaned down to shout above the blaring band. Right in his ear. "Are you a *sojur,* too? Like my daddy?"

"I am." Still felt like he was.

"What's your name?"

"Bryce. What's yours?"

"Gina."

That's what he'd figured. He'd always remember the call from Keith announcing her arrival. How excited he was. How much he considered her a personal gift from God. How he wanted a dozen more just like her. Bryce had hardly been able to get a word in edgewise even to congratulate him.

Gina pointed. "Look! Horses!"

Sure enough, following the band and pom-pommed high school cheerleaders came a mounted Kara Dixon and ex-rodeo cowboy Trey Kenton leading two dozen other riders in Western garb. Saddle leather creaking, bits jangling and metal-shod hooves ringing on the hard-topped street, they passed by in style.

"Mac!" a familiar female voice cried out, and he glimpsed Sandi worming her way through the crowd to his grandma's side. "Oh, thank goodness, a familiar face at last. Have you seen Gina? I've been looking all over—"

"Hi, Mommy! I'm up here with Uncle Bryce."

Uncle Bryce?

He turned to catch the displeasure on the face of the pretty, sun-hatted woman. She looked torn, as if wanting to order him to unhand her daughter but mindful of the prime parade-viewing spot the little latecomer managed to nab.

He almost laughed but thought better of it. "Take it easy, Sandi. I told her Keith and I were like brothers. That's why—"

"I see." She tilted her head to look at him with that appealing little mannerism. Was she even aware of it? Know how engaging it was? Especially to a guy who hadn't gone near an attractive single woman in three years.

But no way was he touching Sandi Bradshaw with

a proverbial ten-foot pole. He might be a lot of things, but stupid wasn't one of them.

He did laugh then, and he didn't care when she frowned.

Still smiling, he turned himself and Gina back to the parade just as the historical society's contribution to the day rolled by, a festively decorated buggy pulled by a flashy chestnut. A placard on the back announced the museum's open-for-business holiday hours.

His smile faded. No doubt the economy had played a hand in the downturn in the historical society's finances just as it had for almost every other business in town. But Grandma had given them a too-generous deal that they'd taken advantage of for far too long. Had he been aware of it years earlier, he'd have called a halt to it then, not waited until circumstances dictated a significant dollar increase all at one time. Even then, the escalation likely wouldn't be sufficient for what he needed to do.

Then what?

He shoved uneasy thoughts aside to pat Gina's leg and point out the miniature ponies coming along the parade route. Thirty minutes later, with the last tractor-pulled float rolling out of sight, he turned just as Sandi took a call on her cell phone.

She glanced in his direction and, catching his eye, turned slightly away. "What's up, Fay?"

She listened intently as Gina drummed a light rhythm on the top of his head.

"I'm thrilled for you," she assured the caller, but

she didn't sound convincing to him. "Of course. No, go and have a great time. Don't worry about it."

She dropped her head in resignation for a moment, then took a deep breath, squared her shoulders and stuffed the phone back in her purse. "Let's get going, Gina. Change in plans. We have to cover at the museum this morning, too."

Little fingers stopped their drumming. "But you promised."

"I know I did, sweetheart, but this can't be helped." She looked to Grandma Mae. "Fay just got asked to spend the day with an out-of-town guy she's been dying to date. And earlier this morning Wanda called to say that her daughter's family arrived unexpectedly late last night. What could I say?"

Grandma Mae patted her hand. "You're too soft-hearted, Sandi."

The pretty blonde grimaced.

Gina wiggled atop his shoulders. "Can't we go to the petting zoo first, Mommy? Please?"

"There's not enough time. We're going to be late opening the museum as it is."

"But Mommy—"

"We can take her, can't we, Bryce?" Grandma smiled up at him. "I haven't been to a petting zoo in years."

Gina clapped her hands as he lowered her to the ground. "Can they take me, Mommy?"

"Well…" She cast him an uncertain glance. Conscious of Grandma's enthusiasm, he didn't shake his head, but he probably had "no" written all over his face. With any luck, she'd take the hint.

Grandma all but glowed. "We'd love to take her."

There was that *we* stuff again.

With a squeal, the kid grasped his hand with both of hers, holding on for dear life as she danced in place, little pink lights on her tennis shoes flashing with every step. Somebody had already consumed way too much sugar this morning.

This isn't a good idea, Grandma.

"That's sweet of you, Mae." Sandi glanced at him again—apparently not sold on the idea of leaving her kid in his care—then back at Grandma. "But only if you're sure it wouldn't be too much trouble."

"We were going to spend most of the day together," Sandi continued with a regretful smile in the direction of her still-dancing daughter. "But now I'm stuck with every single one of the scheduled museum slots."

He shifted his weight, primed to step in if she started complaining about the rent increase in front of Grandma. About how she had to give up her holiday with her kid to bring in more money to cover it.

"Then it's settled." Grandma beamed from Sandi, to Gina, to him.

With another squeal the little girl hugged his leg. "Come on, Uncle Bryce. Let's roll!"

Conscious of her eyes on him, he met the troubled gaze of the too-pretty-for-*his*-own-good young mother. Her lips parted as if she wanted to say something more.

Instead she turned to Grandma, that too-appealing mouth ever so slowly curving into a grateful smile. One that grabbed him by the throat tighter than the grip her kid had on his hand.

He took a steadying breath.

No, Grandma, this isn't a good idea.

Chapter Five

꧁

"Your husband was a handsome man," one of the women from Utah said, nodding to the photograph of a uniformed Keith adorning the local veterans display at the Canyon Springs Historical Museum.

"He was a good one, too." While bittersweet, Sandi always enjoyed pointing out the photos and memorabilia of men and women who'd served in the armed forces. Each time it renewed her determination that the exhibit would be significantly expanded—and dedicated to Keith Bradshaw.

His mother would be so surprised.

And so proud.

She'd finally realize her daughter-in-law had been worthy of her youngest son.

"Don't know what this world would do without men and women willing to make a supreme sacrifice for others," a second woman said softly. "And thank you for answering our questions about the area. I'm still amazed that this oasis of cool pines exists in Arizona. I had no idea."

When they'd departed, the last visitors of the day, Sandi locked the front door then headed to the roll-top desk and pulled out a cash box. At a two-dollar donation per visitor, a "take" for the day of fifty-four dollars might seem, to some, time not well spent. Holiday-goers must have wanted to be outdoors enjoying the weather, just as a number of historical society members who'd declined to assist today had pointed out. But every bit helped keep the museum afloat, so she wouldn't beat herself up about it.

She slipped the cash into a small plastic bag and stuffed it in her purse for a Tuesday bank deposit, then paused to let her gaze travel around the museum's main room. Originally a living room when Bryce's grandparents first moved there, it was now packed with mementos of Canyon Springs's past. Her eyes lingered on the veterans display in the corner.

On Keith's photo.

I'm going to make you and your mom proud. I promise.

"Come on, Gina," she called as she slung her purse over her shoulder. "Gather your things and let's get out of here."

When Mae had returned with Gina after lunch—also bringing Sandi a still-warm gyro from a street vendor—she'd settled her daughter in the kitchen with books, games and crayons.

How she hated being in Bryce's debt for helping

her make up for the lost mom-and-daughter day. But when Mae offered to brighten Gina's morning, how could she refuse? Even with that big boulder of a guy almost glowering at her, she couldn't decline the offer. It was clear he thought she'd try to make his grandma feel bad about raising the museum rent, but he needn't have worried about that. She knew who the guilty party was—and it wasn't Mae.

"Come on, Gina. Let's go."

She pushed open the swinging door to the kitchen. Crayons littered the white-painted wooden table. A ladder-back chair, Gina's jacket draped over it, had been pushed to the side. But no sign of the six-year-old. She headed back to the front of the house, then through the adjoining rooms.

"Gina?"

Now where had she gotten off to? She glanced up the narrow staircase to the apartment above. Could she have gone to see Mae? She knew not to bother her. And wouldn't Sandi have heard the old steps creak even if she'd attempted to sneak up there?

She returned to the kitchen. The glass-paned back door appeared slightly ajar. Ah. She opened it wide, expecting to see Gina on the porch.

Uneasiness niggled. Gina knew better than to wander off. They'd been over the stranger-danger stuff enough times. Sandi stepped outside and walked between the towering ponderosa pines to peek around both sides of the old stone house.

She raised her voice. "Gina!"

Just as she was about to scale the exterior wooden steps to Mae's apartment, she heard a squealing laugh. Gina's laugh. Coming from behind the old garage. With a prayer of thanks, she hurried to the back of the property.

Rounding the corner of the structure, she halted. There in a metal fishing boat mounted on a trailer sat Bryce and Gina—her daughter in the bow and Bryce in the stern—both laughing and rowing away with imaginary oars for all they were worth.

Gina spied her immediately and waved her ball cap. "Mommy! Look! Uncle Bryce has a boat. He can take us fishing."

Fishing? That wasn't something high on her list of favorite things to do. And what was this *Uncle* Bryce stuff again?

She turned to him and his face reddened. He must feel as silly as he looked. Although kind of cute, too. A grown-up guy rowing away with gusto against make-believe waves just to make a little girl giggle.

Laying his "oars" aside, he stood, then jumped out of the boat. Graceful landing for such a big guy. What was he? Six-two? Three? His dark eyes met hers with uncertainty. "She wanted to try it out. I hope that was okay."

"Next time—" she folded her arms, keeping her expression as straight as she could "—don't forget the life jackets."

He stared at her a moment, processing her words,

then a grin split the handsome, bearded face. "Yes, ma'am. My oversight."

A smile tugged at her own lips as their gazes held a little too long. Heart quickening, Sandi turned again to her daughter.

"Let's go, Gina."

The little girl's lower lip protruded. "I want to go fishing, Mommy."

"I don't think so, honey."

"Davy's grandpa and daddy take him fishing."

"Maybe you can go with them sometime."

Gina gripped the edges of the bench seat on each side of her. "I want to go with Uncle Bryce. He's going *now.*"

"Now?" She glanced at Bryce for confirmation.

He nodded.

Helpless in the face of her daughter's obstinacy, she gave him a warning look. *Come on, big guy, give me a hand here since this is your doing.*

Obediently, he reached out to Gina and she went willingly into his arms to be lifted from the boat. "I'm afraid I don't have any little-kid life jackets, Gina. Just big people's."

He set her feet gently on the ground, but she turned to cling to his hand. "You can buy a little people one, can't you?"

Inwardly Sandi cringed. Was her daughter drawn to him, to any man, because she didn't have one in her life? A daddy?

"Gina, that's enough. Don't badger Mr. Harding."

"But I want—"

"Gina."

The little shoulders slumped, but she didn't release his hand. He gave it a reassuring squeeze.

"What do you say I look around for a kid one, then—"

"That's kind of you, Bryce, but you don't need to do that." And no way was she letting this stranger take her daughter out in a boat, Keith's old buddy or not.

"You can come along, too," he said, as if reading her mind. "I'd never take a kid in a boat without another adult as backup."

"Thanks, but we have plans for the evening."

Gina eyes brightened with curiosity. "We do? What?"

Think fast. She intended a quiet evening and an early bedtime for both of them. Tomorrow was a school day. But at the excited look on her daughter's face, she had to do something to make up for their lost day together—and for the never-ending piano brunch with Grandma yesterday. It had been a trial for an active little girl, to say the least.

"The High Country Equine Center's grand opening," she announced as if that had been her intention all along.

"The horse place?" Gina clapped her hands.

Sandi nodded. She'd give Devon a call. See if her cowboy-crazy sister-in-law wanted to join them.

Bryce studied her, his eyes questioning. "Maybe we can all go fishing another time."

Surely he didn't want to take them fishing any more than she wanted to go. He was being nice to a little kid he felt sorry for. Sorry because she didn't have a daddy—and because her mommy didn't deserve the husband she'd had.

How she hated not knowing how much Keith had shared with him. Not knowing if he sat in judgment of her.

"Come along, Gina. We don't want to be late."

Gina didn't argue, but she turned to Bryce with outstretched hands, inviting him for a hug. He glanced again at Sandi as if seeking permission, then squatted down to envelop Gina in his brawny arms. The tiny girl all but disappeared as they folded around her, her eyes squeezed tight to hug him for all she was worth.

A heaviness settled into Sandi's heart. She'd have to talk to Meg and Joe this week. Maybe Joe wouldn't mind an extra kid tagging along on a fishing trip. Maybe he'd be willing to give Gina a little "man time" to help make her less needy.

Less vulnerable to Uncle Bryce.

Bryce watched them walk away, a lump in his throat. Guilt pierced as he savored the childish embrace that by rights didn't belong to him. What a shame Keith wasn't around to receive precious hugs from the sweet little lady he'd sired. It should be her daddy she was clinging to, not him.

And it should be Keith looking into the eyes of her lovely mother, as well, sharing a smile and a too-long moment of mutual awareness. Letting his gaze linger on her face...

Shaken, he turned back to the boat. He hadn't expected an attraction to Sandi, knowing what he knew about her. It caught him off-guard now, just as it had at the Warehouse, museum and parade. He had no business looking at her like that, thinking about her. Didn't need to be noticing she was a gentle and caring mom. Didn't need to be wondering how hard life had been in the five years since Keith's passing—and about who would look after her and Gina in the years to come.

No, he had to remember this was Keith's wife. The woman who'd lured his unsuspecting buddy down the path to matrimony, then proceeded to dictate to him what the rest of his life would be like—just like Keith's mom had attempted. Just like Bryce's own mother, when she bothered to drop in on his childhood at all, had tried to do. Ordering him around. Imposing her will on his. Never pleased with anything he did.

He squared his shoulders. From now on he'd watch himself. With God's help, he'd keep his mind from wandering off where it didn't belong. He'd come back to town to help Grandma, not to get snared in some pretty woman's web.

He studied the boat. He didn't feel much like packing up his gear and hauling the watercraft out to Casey Lake. Maybe he'd listen to those Bible-study CDs. Complete another online firefighting course assignment.

Or check out the equine center's grand opening.

* * *

Grasping Gina's hand, Sandi followed Devon through the crowded parking lot of the equine center. They'd arrived late and had to park down near the main road, then walk up the tree-lined lane leading to the massive indoor arena and stable. The High Country Equine Center—or "Duffy's" as locals knew it—had been closed for over a decade. But now, under new ownership, expanded and remodeled, it was open for business again. Horse boarding, riding lessons, special events.

"Hurry, Mommy."

Gina skipped along at her side, the oversize cap sitting crookedly on her head. The begged-for fishing trip seemed long forgotten as the evening air filled with shrill whinnies and the scent of sun-warmed pine, wood shavings, hay and horses.

Even Sandi's own spirits lifted as she joined the excited throng of summer folks and locals. Always grateful when the crowds dispersed in the autumn, she nevertheless got caught up in the invigorating energy the annual influx of both familiar and unfamiliar faces brought with it. Seeking refuge in the ponderosa pine-studded community with its cool, more-than-a-mile-high elevation, the desert dwellers were the lifeblood of the economic health of Canyon Springs—and the museum.

"I had no idea this was such a big deal," confided Devon. Nevertheless, she'd gone all out with a pricey brand of boot-cut jeans and a sparkly red shirt. Even sported cowboy boots and a sassy feather-accented Western hat. Knowing she couldn't compete with her fashion-savvy sister-in-law, Sandi had stuck with Levi's, a T-shirt and tennis shoes.

Over the sound system a booming voice of welcome sounded like Kara Dixon's fiancé, Trey Kenton, who now managed the facility. The opening notes of the national anthem soon followed.

Gina tugged on her hand. "Hurry."

The threesome wove their way among other late-comers, paid their way in and slipped through the opening to the arena seating. The place was packed. They should have come straight here, not gone home to have dinner and wait for Devon.

"Way up there, Mommy. I see seats!"

With a laugh and a shrug in Devon's direction, she let Gina lead the way. Her daughter scrambled up the bleacher steps as Sandi followed behind. Sliding in sideways, focusing on maintaining her balance and apologizing for treading on toes, she and Devon kept an eye on Gina moving down one of the rows ahead of them. The little girl finally plopped on a gap of empty bleacher space, then grinned back at them.

"See? Uncle Bryce saved us seats."

Sandi's gaze flew to the man seated next to Gina, his hand raised to the brim of his straw cowboy hat in greeting. Wouldn't you know it. A huge arena holding hundreds upon hundreds and Gina had to find a spot next to him.

"*Uncle* Bryce?" whispered Devon, securing her hat

with her hand and pressing in close to Sandi's ear. "Woo-hoo, gal. You didn't waste any time, did you?"

Sandi ignored her. Motioning to the open spaces, her eyes locked uncertainly on Bryce's. "Are you saving these for anyone?"

"Just for three of the prettiest cowgirls I've seen tonight. Have a seat, ladies."

Gina giggled and Devon poked Sandi in the back.

Reluctantly, she sat beside her daughter, and Devon squished in on Sandi's other side. Wiggling to find a comfortable spot, she bumped Sandi and Gina even closer to Bryce.

What was Bryce doing here anyway? Wasn't he supposed to be fishing? Self-consciously, she glanced at the sea of spectators surrounding her. Most focused on the palominos with silver-studded tack galloping around the arena, cream-colored tails flying as their riders wove in and out of figure eights. Most paid attention to the spectacle in front of them—except an auburn-haired woman several rows down pointedly looking from Sandi to Bryce to Gina and back again.

Sandi reluctantly acknowledged her with a finger wave.

Cate Landreth. A teacher's aide at the high school, historical society member and rumormonger extraordinaire. Had Cate been close enough to hear Gina's shouted labeling of Bryce as "uncle"? She'd talked to Gina about that on the way home this afternoon. Explained that Bryce wasn't her uncle. But she insisted he was like a brother to her daddy. And wasn't daddy's big brother, Lance, her *Uncle* Lance? And Scott, *Uncle* Scott? Nevertheless, she'd asked Gina not to call him that in public.

But she'd forgotten.

"Hi, Bryce." Devon leaned across her, hand outstretched. "You remember me, don't you?"

He studied her a moment, then recognition dawned and a smile broadened as he shook her hand. "Keith's little sister, Devon. All grown up."

"Hey, you're good. I think I was about eight years old the last time you saw me."

Bryce nodded thoughtfully. "That would be about right. Before Keith and I joined the army. But he always showed off pictures of his family. You resemble him, but a lot prettier."

They chitchatted a few minutes, then Devon settled back into her seat and Bryce returned his gaze to the arena.

"He is so hot," Devon breathed into Sandi's ear as she discreetly fanned her face with her hand. "Forget what Mom says. Keith wouldn't pick a jerk for a best friend."

Sandi wasn't so sure about that.

Gina climbed onto her lap and, as another woman slipped in on the far side of Devon, her sister-in-law shifted once again, pushing Sandi to within an inch of Bryce.

She glanced up to see him gazing at her, his forehead creased in a frown. Her face warmed. He probably thought she was making inappropriate advances.

Keith's wife on the prowl for husband number two. *In his dreams.* She gave Devon a discreet shove with her hip and gained another inch between her and the ex-military man.

Nevertheless, with Gina wiggling on her lap, occasionally her arm brushed his. And each time her breath caught. How could she concentrate on the performance with him next to her? Maybe she should leave Gina with Devon and go hide in the ladies' room until the whole thing was over.

"He can't keep his eyes off you." Devon's whisper came again. "Tell him how big and strong and masculine he looks tonight. Men love that. Feeds their egos. You'll have him eating out of your hand."

Sandi shifted and "accidentally" elbowed her sister-in-law, but nevertheless managed to cast a discreet look in Bryce's direction. He wasn't looking at her as Devon claimed. But she could admit *he* sure was nice to look at. Strong profile. Expressive eyes.

He'd been so nice to Gina, too.

That was the reason she found him somewhat attractive, right? A man who's good to your kid—even if he did think you'd make a lousy wife to his best friend—made him appear more good-looking than he really was. Kind of put a golden glow around him. Besides, merely finding someone—anyone—attractive didn't mean there was an actual *attraction* there.

Still conscious of his proximity, she refocused on the arena, reminding herself this was the man who'd single-handedly managed to keep her from honor-

ing her husband with a museum exhibit by summer's
end. The man who'd done his best to talk Keith out of
marrying her. Who'd shortchanged them out of who
knows how many months they could have shared
before her husband's death. Who'd cheated her of an
opportunity to make things turn out differently.

Very differently.

"Say something to him." Devon's voice again tickled her ear and Sandi shifted to get away from her.
Bumped against Bryce. He looked over at her, and her
face warmed again. *Please, Lord, get me out of this.*

Bryce leaned toward her bright-eyed daughter.
"Would you like a hot dog? Popcorn? Snow cone?"

Gina twisted to face her. "Can I, Mom?"

"Okay. But only one thing."

"Snow cone! Grape."

Gina beamed at Bryce, and Sandi's gaze once again
met his, caught off-guard by the kindness in his eyes.
"Thank you."

"You're welcome. You want anything?"

Yes. To be a million miles from here.

She shook her head, and he nodded toward Devon.
"How about you? Anything you want?"

She could almost hear the inappropriate thoughts
simmering in Devon's head, but Keith's sister smiled
primly. "A Coke, please."

He nodded, placed his hat on the seat next to Sandi
and headed to the concession stand.

Thank You, Lord.

She gave Gina a grateful hug. Then cast a dirty look at the smirking Devon.

Chapter Six

Man, it had gotten warm in there.

All those people breathing the same air. Crammed in so close. *Sandi snuggling in even closer.* Bryce pulled a handkerchief from a back pocket and wiped his forehead as he waited for his order at the concession. He'd had to get out of there, at least for a while.

"Hello, Bryce."

He turned to an auburn-haired woman, Cate Landreth, who'd been behind him in school. He'd run into her and her husband a time or two since returning to town. She always seemed friendly enough, but he hadn't much taken to her.

"I see you're with Sandi Bradshaw tonight."

He wasn't *with* Sandi, but he supposed it looked like that, with her sitting all cozied up next to him, her daughter in her lap. Like a threesome. But there wasn't any point in explaining all that to someone he didn't know well.

"I've always said she's a mighty bright gal." Cate

darted a look at him, as if she knew a secret she was dying to share. "This proves it."

Was he missing something here? "How's that?"

"The museum rent." She stared at him as though he was thicker than a stand of old-growth ponderosa. "Tourist fees sure ain't going to make up the difference. Everybody knows it, but Sandi's not one to give up, God bless her. And we sure would hate to lose the museum." She winked. "*Uncle* Bryce."

The woman laughed, gave him a wave and sauntered off.

What was she implying? That Sandi planned to butter him up? Intended to use her feminine wiles to talk him out of the rent increase? Was that what tonight was all about? She'd managed to hone in on his location in the midst of hundreds of people with all the accuracy of a GPS. Then all the furtive looks, distracting movements, sweet blushes. Had she coached her daughter to keep calling him Uncle Bryce, too?

He should have known.

Hadn't he learned anything at all from Keith's involvement with the manipulative little minx? If he didn't watch it, he'd be falling off the same cliff his buddy had.

No way would he let that happen.

No way.

"Wouldn't you like to move to Paradise Valley, Gina?" LeAnne placed a hand on her granddaughter's shoulder as they walked to the trailer in the fading light and stepped up on the front deck. With school letting out for the summer the previous Wednesday, they'd been to an early Friday evening Disney flick and a fast-food dinner. Now they were home for dessert. "Wouldn't you like to live with Grandma?"

"I want to live with Mommy." Gina looked at her mother, uncertainty in her eyes.

Sandi shot her a reassuring smile, hoping it reminded her of earlier discussions that calmed fears of Grandma uprooting her from Canyon Springs.

LeAnne laughed and pulled Gina close for a hug, avoiding looking at Sandi. "Of course you do. Mommy can come, too. Wouldn't that be fun?"

Scads.

LeAnne wouldn't let up. For the past five years she'd badgered Sandi to relocate to the Valley. To abandon Canyon Springs and allow Gina more "opportunities" a city could offer. She even pressed to have Keith's body moved from its pine-shaded resting place to the Bradshaw family mausoleum in the desert.

But recently she'd started in on Gina about a move, as well, even though she'd been asked not to persist. When Sandi reminded her last month, explaining how it made Gina feel anxious, LeAnne acted taken aback, insisting she was "just teasing."

She unlocked the front door and held it open for the other two to enter. "We're quite happy right where we are, aren't we, Gina?"

Her daughter gave her an enthusiastic nod, the

creases in her forehead brought on by her grandma's questions evaporating. "This is the bestest place in the whole wide world."

"You might be surprised, Gina," LeAnne continued as she and her granddaughter seated themselves at the oval kitchen table, "at what else is out there in that world you've never seen."

Sandi forced a smile as she moved to a cabinet for bowls. "I think she has plenty of time yet to explore it."

Ironically, there was a time she would have given anything to be living anywhere but Canyon Springs— although not with her mother-in-law, thank you very much. Keith had been so sold on the little town where he'd spent his summers as a kid that he'd wasted no time settling his bride in his fishing hideaway. She hadn't been happy about it nor had she been shy about vocalizing her displeasure. But now this is exactly where she wanted to be for Gina's sake.

For Keith's.

She turned to her daughter. "Why don't you run and get that picture you drew for Grandma? The one of the horse show."

Gina hopped up off her chair and ran down the short hallway to her bedroom.

Saying a prayer for courage, she took a deep breath. "LeAnne—"

"I know you don't want to hear it, Sandi." The older woman folded her arms. "But Keith wouldn't want you and Gina to continue living here."

Sandi opened the freezer and pulled out a gallon of ice cream. Retrieved the metal scoop from a drawer. "This is where he wanted to raise Gina. I intend to honor his wishes."

"That may have been his initial plan, darling, to come back to a town filled with carefree childhood memories. Goodness knows he'd gravitate to anything that would help him forget war." She tapped on the table with a fingernail. "But the reality of living in a tiny town like this—in a dumpy little trailer—would have worn thin."

Dumpy? Her cozy Bradshaws-in-the-Pines was dumpy? Little did LeAnne know that it was far nicer than the cramped apartment where she'd grown up in Kansas City.

Her mother-in-law's tone softened to its most persuasive. "I have no doubt he'd have soon come to his senses. Would have left the army, relocated his family, gotten his law degree."

Wordlessly, Sandi dipped ice cream into the bowls. Yes, there was a time, unknown to LeAnne, that she'd been on her mother-in-law's side of this issue—but for a totally different reason. She'd been certain Keith's determination to settle here had been nothing more than remnants of the parental rebellion that had driven him to follow Bryce into the armed forces. To ditch his coveted Harvard scholarship. To kiss goodbye the guaranteed position at the generations-old family law firm and a lifetime of public service to the state of Arizona.

But she couldn't go along with LeAnne now, not even if moving to the Valley of the Sun would win brownie points. This was one of the few things on which she'd quietly stood her ground. Once the museum featured a veterans exhibit dedicated to Keith, surely her mother-in-law would bestow praise for sticking with her husband's original plan.

"Don't get me wrong," LeAnne hurried on, "Canyon Springs is a dear, sweet town—for a holiday. But to settle in forever?"

"I know it's hard to understand, but—"

A rattling knock came at the door. Gina dashed out of her bedroom, a piece of drawing paper flapping in her hand. "I'll get it!"

She opened the door wide, and a familiar, broad-shouldered male form filled the doorway.

"Mommy! It's Uncle Bryce!"

Sandi didn't have to look at LeAnne to know a questioning stare bored into her. She joined Gina at the door as Bryce handed something to her little girl.

Eyes wide, Gina took the sand-colored fabric object from his hand and clutched both it and her drawing to her heart. "Mommy, look! He found Daddy's hat."

Gina hadn't noticed the cap missing until after school let out on Wednesday. They'd looked everywhere for it. Even driven back to the building and searched because she couldn't remember when she'd last worn it.

Relieved beyond measure, Sandi gave Bryce a grateful smile. "Where on earth did you find it?"

"At the arena Monday night. Under the seats after you left. Sorry I didn't return it sooner. Tucked it up under the passenger-side sun visor and forgot about it until tonight."

"Thank you, Uncle Bryce." Gina grasped him around the legs for a hug. "I love you."

Startled, he met Sandi's gaze with an apologetic look, as if somehow he was undeserving of her child's adoration.

"She loves that hat," she assured him. In fact, when Gina realized she'd lost it, no amount of hugs and kisses consoled her. She'd cried herself to sleep that first night. "You've made a little girl very, very happy."

Should she invite him in? Ask him to join them for ice cream? LeAnne was here, still staring razor-sharp daggers at her no doubt. To hear her mother-in-law tell it, Bryce had been a brat of the first order and a bad influence on Keith. But he was her husband's best friend. And this was *her* home. And Gina's. Bryce had gone out of his way when he didn't have to.

Still debating, she caught an unexpected appreciative flicker of his gaze to her bare, shorts-clad legs. Her face warmed. On second thought, maybe he'd better be on his way.

"Can Uncle Bryce have ice cream with us, Mommy?"

Guess that settled it.

"You have to join us. It's the least we can do to reward you for being Gina's hero."

"Oh, yes, by all means join us." LeAnne's coolish tones carried from the table across the room. "*Uncle Bryce.*"

He'd barely knocked at the door and already had three Bradshaw females telling him what to do.

He hadn't spotted LeAnne when the kid opened the door. He'd flunked his reconnaissance training bigtime, focusing only on the two winsome ladies who'd greeted him. He pulled off his Western hat and nodded in the direction of Keith's mom as he stepped into the trailer.

"Nice to see you again, Mrs. Bradshaw."

Would God strike him dead for saying that?

"Likewise."

Right. And he was only two-foot-four.

Sandi clasped her hands, then motioned him toward the dining area. "Have a seat. I'm just dishing it up."

"Thanks, but I really can't—"

"You gotta stay, Uncle Bryce. It's chocolate chip." Gina plunked her dad's cap on her head and grabbed his hand.

He looked at Sandi. Did she want him to stay? He'd rather not. Not with LeAnne here. And not after that Landreth woman at the equine center Monday night hinted Sandi was attempting to get on his good side.

"Gina picked out the flavor all by herself."

Sandi's eyes encouraged, and his resolve wavered.

"Chocolate chip, huh?"

"Please?" The little girl tugged at his hand, and against his better judgment he gave in. Didn't want to disappoint her. But oh, man, he hadn't dined with LeAnne since Keith had dragged him home on rare occasions to her fancy gated community during high school. Even after all this time, the memories were still too vivid to make him feel good about this.

It was akin to walking in front of a firing squad.

But he was a changed man now. *Right, Lord?* Maybe she'd changed, too.

He followed Sandi and Gina into the dining area and placed his hat on the counter. Then he pulled out a chair as far from LeAnne as he could get and took in his surroundings. Nice place. Wasn't at all what he'd have expected of Keith's wife, though. While it was simple and uncluttered, it remained comfortable. Inviting. Family photos. Soft lighting. Not at all an impersonal, coldly modern look as he would have assumed had he taken time to think about it.

Interesting.

Sandi opened the dining area's sliding glass door, letting in the now-cooling twilight air. A cricket chirped from somewhere on the back deck as Gina distributed bowls of ice cream and spoons. Then mother and daughter seated themselves on each side of him as he counted the seconds, wondering how long it would be before the first volley fired.

"So, Bryce. You're back in Canyon Springs." LeAnne crossed her forearms and placed them on the edge of the table, pinning him with the same judgmental gaze he remembered from childhood. "Where are you working now?"

A lacquered fingernail tapped on the table. He'd forgotten those glossy, dark-polished nails. Forgotten the sound they made when she tried to make a point. And the point now was that he was pretty much unemployed—and she knew it.

Deliberately relaxing back in his chair, he stirred the ice cream with his spoon. This was practically like old times, except Keith wasn't here to enjoy it. But as much as he'd have liked to set the woman straight with a flippant retort, he had changed. Right? He wouldn't let her bully him back into being the defensive, belligerent kid she undoubtedly remembered.

"I'm tending to my grandma. Working odd jobs and doing volunteer work as I adjust back into civilian life. Then when the time is right, I'll step into something full-time."

"And what might you expect that timing and job to be?"

He scooped up a spoonful of ice cream and smiled. "Afraid I'm not at liberty to say."

She probably thought he was lying, covering up. But it was the truth. The fire chief, an old friend of the family, had been in preliminary negotiations with him last year as he'd neared his discharge from the army. Unfortunately, the anticipated opening fell by the wayside right before he'd arrived in town. Major city budget cutbacks. For various reasons, the p agreed to keep their talks to themselves until monies were once again released.

So for now, he'd have to let Keith's mom think he was freeloading off his grandma. It should make her happy that her oft-shared predictions that he'd never amount to much had come to pass.

"I drawed this, Uncle Bryce." Gina held up a wrinkled piece of construction paper and held it out to him.

"Wow. Look at this." *Give me a hint, kid. What is it?*

"You're holding it upside down." She plucked it from his fingers and turned it the other way.

"I knew that."

Gina rolled her eyes, then downed another spoonful of ice cream. "I made it for Grandma so she could see the horse show. But you can have it."

He glanced at LeAnne, sitting tight-lipped, her ice cream untouched. He slid the paper across the table toward the older woman. "Thanks, Gina, but I'm sure your grandma has a special place for it."

Sandi shifted in her chair. "So, Bryce, how is Mae doing? I intended to stop in and see her this week, but things kept coming up one right after another."

"Things like putting in more hours at that museum, I imagine." LeAnne's words scolded her daughter-in-law, but her attention riveted on him. "Such a shame that the rent's being raised when you finally have free time to spend with Gina. Devon said you worked all day Monday."

"Couldn't be helped," Sandi said lightly, passing a napkin to Gina so she could wipe the ice cream from her face.

"Grandma Mae and Uncle Bryce took me to the petting zoo," Gina chimed in. "And Uncle Bryce is going to take me fishing."

He nearly laughed at the way LeAnne's lip curled in distaste. But whether at the fishing or Uncle Bryce reference—or both—was a toss-up.

Sandi gave her daughter a "look." "You know that hasn't been decided. You may be going with Davy and his dad."

"I want to go with Uncle Bryce. He has a boat."

Keith's mom again fixed her eyes on him. So much for Gina's innocent diversionary tactic.

"So Bryce, what are you planning to do with those additional museum funds?"

Amazing how some things never changed. *You're missing out, Keith, old buddy.* He bestowed her a serene smile he knew she'd find irritating. "Thought I'd spend a few months in the Bahamas. You're welcome to join me."

Now where'd that come from? Old Bryce. The smart aleck who hated being pushed into a corner, especially by Keith's mom. Or any woman other than his grandma for that matter.

"Where's the *Mahamas?*" Gina licked her spoon. "Can I go, too?"

LeAnne's eyebrows rose ever so slightly, then

turned to her granddaughter. "Gina, dear. Why don't you take your hat off while you're at the table. Your *Uncle* Bryce thinks your mother didn't teach you any manners."

Bryce bristled at the uncalled-for slur on Sandi's parenting but, unfazed by her grandma's reprimand, a grinning Gina pulled off the cap and leaned over to plop it on top of *his* head. Much too small, of course, with the band adjusted as tight as it could go for the little girl. He knew he looked silly, and he reached over to poke her gently in the side. She giggled and squirmed, then both caught her grandma's disapproving eye. Exchanging a mischievous look with Gina, Bryce placed the hat on the table between them and they both settled down to their ice cream.

Cute kid. Keith's mom hadn't yet managed to squash her spunk. He glanced at Sandi. She'd probably held up fine, too, under her mother-in-law's dictatorial ways. The pair had been on the same page when it came to how Keith should live his life, so there must be some kind of bond between the two in spite of LeAnne's parenting dig.

The older woman pushed back her ice cream bowl. "It's a bit too chilly tonight for ice cream."

"I'm sorry. I shouldn't have opened the door." Sandi cast her mother-in-law an anxious look. "I thought since you're used to air-conditioning that it might seem too warm in here."

Sandi got to her feet to close it, but LeAnne's outstretched hand stayed her. "Don't bother, dear. I need to get on home."

Was this where he should say something like "don't hurry off because of me" or "I should be going, too?" But he kept his mouth shut and concentrated on his ice cream as LeAnne retrieved her purse, kissed the top of her granddaughter's head and moved to the front door with Sandi right behind her.

No goodbye for him.

He could hear the murmured voices of the two women. LeAnne's brisk tones. Her pointed "I'll call you."

He'd go home, too, as soon as she left.

As soon as he'd finished his ice cream.

Just as soon as he confirmed Sandi intended to smooth talk him into rethinking the museum business.

Chapter Seven

Leaning the side of her head against the doorjamb, Sandi watched her mother-in-law—illuminated by the porch light—make her way safely to her car. Its head-lights came on as it started, then the vehicle moved down the darkened road.

Well, that had been more than awkward.

Now she had Bryce camped out in her kitchen. She owed him an apology. What was with LeAnne tonight? But although she herself was curious about Bryce's job prospects and his intentions for the museum funds, LeAnne had been so rude about it. Flat-out bad-mannered wasn't usually her style.

"I need to get going, too."

Startled, she spun in the direction of the low, mas-culine voice. Looked up into the dark eyes of the bearded man standing right behind her, toying with the Western hat in his hands. Sneaky for such a big guy, which probably paid off in a war zone.

She took a step back and bumped awkwardly into the door frame. He caught her arm in a gentle grasp to steady her, and their gazes connected once again.

He released her arm and together, as if by mutual agreement, they stepped out on the deck, letting the door close behind them.

Her words came softly so Gina wouldn't hear. "I'm sorry about the way Keith's mom acted tonight."

Bryce kept his own volume turned down, too. "You're not responsible for her. I'm afraid we never hit it off. Keith probably told you about my background. Why it didn't meet her standards?"

"Some."

"Well, as you can imagine, a kid who didn't even know who his father was and whose mother flitted in and out of his life didn't meet LeAnne's prerequisites for friendship with her son."

"I'm sorry." According to Keith, his mom had gone to great lengths to separate the two boys. That's what instigated the move to a gated community when they were teens. But by then it was too late. A lasting bond had been formed.

Bryce shrugged. "It's not like I imagined the two of us becoming buds after Keith's death. But I have to admit I'm disappointed she still believes it's her ordained role to keep me in my place. I thought she might have changed, but obviously she hasn't."

She gazed up at him, unable to curtail her curiosity. "What about you? Have *you* changed?"

He chuckled, and she couldn't help returning his smile.

"I have. In a big way, even though sometimes it may not be apparent—not even to me. But I can admit as a kid I lived to ruffle her feathers. Keith considered it entertainment second to none. Egged me on."

"He did?"

"It may be hard to believe, but the Keith you knew and the Keith I grew up with weren't one and the same."

"You mean because he got his life on track with God before I met him?"

The twinkle in his eyes muted. "When you live daily with the reality that someone's trying to kill you, you can go one of two ways. Get right with your creator or shake your fist at Him. Keith just wised up long before I did."

"But you did?"

He nodded, his eyes meeting hers in solemn acknowledgment. "Took losing Keith to get me to unclench my fist."

His revelation caught her off-guard, a million questions racing to the tip of her tongue. But Bryce placed his hat on his head and took a step toward the deck's stairs as if that was as far as he intended to go on that topic.

"Guess I'll see you around, Sandi."

"Thank you again for bringing Keith's hat back to Gina."

"Happy to do it. And when you're ready to take her fishing, the boat and tackle are at your service."

"I'm afraid I'm not much of a fisherman." Keith had tried to persuade her to join him during a leave of absence. She'd turned him down flat. Had her husband no clue he'd married a girly girl? Besides, she could barely swim.

But now she wished she'd gone, mermaid or not.

"Not a whole lot to it. Bait the hook. Drop it in the water. Sit back and relax."

Relax? Trapped in a boat out in the middle of a lake with Bryce? "I'm sure there's more to it than that."

"You can find out for yourself. Gina, too."

Why was he persisting in this? For Gina's sake, because he knew how much she wanted to go? "Thanks, but—"

The front door opened and Gina peeked out. "Are you leaving, Uncle Bryce?"

"Sure am. What's that on your face?"

Grinning, Gina put her hands on her hips. "Grandma's ice cream."

Dismayed not only by the smear on her face but the chocolate chip dollop on her T-shirt, Sandi shook her head—and again her gaze grazed Bryce's amused one. Her breath quickened.

Just go. Get on out of here. Git.

Shoo. Scat.

But he didn't seem in much of a hurry. Took his

own sweet time saying his goodbyes to Gina, crouching for a hug she insisted on giving him.

When he finally departed, Sandi turned off the porch light and scooted Gina to the bathroom to wash her off. Helped her into her pajamas—a bigger-than-usual challenge because Gina didn't want to take off her daddy's cap.

"Mommy? Does Uncle Bryce have little kids?"

"I don't think so, honey. Why?"

"He needs little kids." She emphasized her matter-of-fact words with a nod of her head.

"Why's that?"

"Because he's a good daddy." Gina gave her a hug and headed to her room to await a bedtime story.

Sandi lingered for a few moments straightening the bathroom as she mulled over Bryce's words—how he'd unclenched his fist. And Gina's comment about him being daddy material. Would her daughter ask for a daddy-and-the-guinea-pigs story tonight?

Or an Uncle-Bryce-and-the-fishing-boat one?

Big dumb ox.

He thought he'd known what she was up to, thanks to Cate Landreth at the horse show clueing him in. Yet that night at Sandi's place he'd lingered at the front door. Invited her—again—to join him on a fishing trip. Keith had once told him she'd refused to go with him, so he wanted to see just how far she'd take it to get on his good side.

But she hadn't swallowed the, um, bait.

Now here it was a week later and he had to admit that unless you counted the sideways glances he'd intercepted at the horse show and at her place, he didn't see anything he'd label as putting a "move" on him to get him to change his mind about the rent. He'd had women put moves on him plenty of times before, so he had a good idea of what that might entail. To his shame, the possibility kind of caught Old Bryce's fancy as something he might have some fun with. But obviously the woman who'd tipped him off had it all wrong.

So why'd he keep thinking about Sandi? Sure as shootin', it didn't appear she was thinking about him. She hadn't said a word, either, when he mentioned Keith's death had driven him to God. Probably didn't believe it. Couldn't blame her.

"What are you doing inside on a nice day like this?" Grandma Mae poked him in the shoulder as she made her way past where he sat at the kitchen table with his netbook open in front of him. She'd just gotten up from a nap.

"Checking email." And running covert calculations on the current state of their finances. The minutes were ticking before a decision about what to do with the second-floor apartment had to be made.

For the time being, Grandma had agreed not to navigate on her own the outside back stairs leading to the apartment or the ones inside through the historical museum below. He could stick close by right now, with his part-time jobs and volunteer work at the fire department. Could drop in to check on her throughout the day. But when he got that firefighter position, he'd be gone for weeks at the fire academy. Then after that he could be called out in the middle of the night or be away for days.

He scanned the spreadsheet columns again. That increase in the rent couldn't kick in any too soon.

At least Grandma hadn't argued, as he expected she might, when he suggested they look for a part-time caregiver, a nurse to check in on her, help her with personal self-care that was awkward for a grandson. Someone who could be available at a moment's notice if Bryce had to be away.

Gran had balked, however, at the necessity of raising the rent on the Canyon Springs Historical Museum to cover some of the other plans he had for her. But eventually she'd been convinced that the figure she'd quoted to the society fifteen years ago was now laughable.

"Earth to Bryce." Grandma waved a hand in front of his face. "You should get out more. Big strapping boy like you needs some activity."

"I'm getting plenty of that digging postholes for Trey Kenton down at the equine center. You know, to fence that piece of forested property that burned a dozen or so years back. He's had all the old stumps removed and will reseed it for pasture."

He'd been unloading and stacking hay bales for Trey, too. And jogging every day to acclimate to the more-than-mile-high elevation. He didn't want to fall on his face during the firefighter physical qualifications.

Grandma turned to lean back against the countertop. "I'm talking recreational exercise. You haven't been fishing since Memorial Day weekend."

He grinned. "You're thinking lifting that fishing pole will keep me in top shape?"

"Fishing's good exercise for the soul. But now that you mention it, guess I don't want you getting all flabby on me, either. I'm still praying you'll catch the eye of some local gal so I can have great-grandkids before I depart this world."

Jarred by her words—this was the first time she'd voiced anything like that—his thoughts flew unbidden to one local gal in particular. Glossy blond hair. Trim figure. Sweet smile. A bit on the bossy side at times.

He pushed Sandi's captivating image away. No point in inviting any more trouble into his life.

"Not making you any promises on that one, Gran." But he *had* promised to do his best to help her retain her independence as long as he could. Grandpa died when Bryce was seven and Grandma moved them upstairs, then rented out the first floor—eventually to the historical society. So if that meant him sleeping on the sofa in the tiny living room, just as he had when growing up, so be it. And if it meant raising the museum rent to supplement remodeling the downstairs so she could have accessible living quarters, he'd do that, too.

"Well, then, at least make yourself useful. Go pick up one of those corn bread mixes and a bag of Anasazi beans for me. That'll be our dinner tonight. Anasazis don't have to soak too many hours before cooking."

"Who carries them?"

"Only place I know is the Warehouse."

"You want me to go right now?" It was only one o'clock in the afternoon. Sandi would still be working her shift. As near as he'd been able to determine, once school had let out she'd been covering the noon to 4:00 p.m. hours several days a week.

Not that he'd been keeping track.

But had Grandma?

"I'm sorry, LeAnne, but I can't chat right now. A few customers just came in. But I wanted to let you know not to expect us this evening."

"You're not coming for pizza?"

"Something came up at the last minute."

"We've always gotten together on Friday evenings."

Each summer since Keith's death, Friday nights had been their night. Renting movies. Going out to eat. Watching a ball game at the city park. Attending a community band concert or a family-friendly play at the local theater.

But the change in plans had come unexpectedly, and she didn't dare pass up the opportunity to make her voice heard. Not if what Cate Landreth had told her was true. Her presence might make all the difference—if it wasn't too late already.

LeAnne's voice sharpened. "You're going out with Bryce Harding, aren't you?"

"Why would you think that?" Sandi hadn't spoken to him since last week. Thought about him maybe. Wondered where he'd been keeping himself.

"I saw the way he looked at you the night he showed up on your doorstep. I'm not so old that I don't recognize male interest when I see it. He's getting to you through Gina. Hero to the rescue with the hat. The Uncle Bryce thing."

"I already explained that." Had, in fact, explained it more than once since LeAnne's regrettable encounter with Bryce. She'd clarified how she didn't have the heart—even as much as she wanted to—to squelch the child's spontaneous outpouring of affection that "uncle" played a part in.

But her mother-in-law still wasn't buying it.

"I'm not seeing Bryce, LeAnne. I haven't so much as talked to him since that night."

"Then why the cancellation?"

She wouldn't like the answer, but at least she'd get her off this Bryce fixation. "There's a special meeting of the city council tonight. I've been told by a somewhat reliable source that with the new fiscal year starting July 1, there may be unanticipated cutbacks announced tonight."

"You're not on the city council."

"No, but I'm a resident of this community and president of the Canyon Springs Historical Society. So if they're contemplating cutting off our funding—as is rumored—I have a right to hear it in person, not in the weekly paper."

"You're getting yourself entirely too wrapped up with this museum business. It's not good for you. Or Gina."

She closed her eyes and took a steadying breath. Why couldn't LeAnne give her a little credit? She wasn't throwing herself into the museum because she didn't have anything better to do. She had a plan. A goal. One that LeAnne would one day come to appreciate. "Keith loved this community, its history, and intended to get involved in the society when he returned."

"But he didn't return, now did he?" LeAnne's voice cracked, and the sound pierced Sandi's soul.

No, he hadn't returned. Would never return.

Was that what this was all about? The suspicion? Accusations? All evidence that LeAnne was having a difficult time with the anniversary of Keith's death, which was only weeks away? She blinked back the moisture in her own eyes, her voice softening. "Let's get together tomorrow instead. Gina and I'll bring pizza after work. We'll spend the night. Okay, LeAnne?"

A choking sob echoed over the line and the phone in her hand went dead.

She let out a shaky gust of pent-up breath and wiped at the corner of her eye. She'd take LeAnne's emotional response to her suggestion as a yes. It sounded as if her usually stalwart mother-in-law needed a heavy dose of TLC. The anniversary of Keith's death always challenged Sandi's own heart, as well, her faith—the latter of which LeAnne didn't have to fall back on.

She hadn't intended to disappoint her. LeAnne, despite their differences, meant so much to her. As Keith's mom, but also as a friend. Sure, they'd gotten off to a rough start, but after his death Sandi had always known, without fail, there would be someone to share an otherwise empty evening. Then when back in Paradise Valley, LeAnne never failed to call on Friday nights to check in on her. Make sure she was okay.

But maybe the connection was as much for LeAnne as it was for her?

Composing herself, she stuffed her cell phone in her purse. Once the customers were checked out, she stepped onto the covered porch that faced Main Street, again noticing how traffic had picked up as desert temperatures a few hours to the south reached well beyond the hundred-degree mark.

A massive RV pulling a car rumbled down the hard-topped road in front of her, probably heading to Bill Diaz's Lazy D Campground and RV Park or one of the other woodsy retreats in the off-the-beaten-path community.

"Good to see them back, isn't it?"

With a start, she spun in the direction of the familiar male voice.

Chapter Eight

◦◦◦

Sandi's heart lifted inexplicably as, with a tilt of his Western hat, Bryce joined her on the plank-floored porch, his muscular arm motioning to the big "land whale" passing by. He grew up here, understood how important summer revenue was to the town.

So he *should* understand how important it was to the museum.

"Visitors are still sparse compared to some years," she pointed out, tamping down her uncharitable thoughts. Being upset about LeAnne and Keith made her more susceptible than usual to negativity, especially when it came to Bryce. "But it's a start. Feels like a carnival's come to town. A little one anyway. Hopefully with extra cash in its pockets."

Bryce nodded agreement, oblivious to her inner turmoil. "You're working this afternoon?"

"Yes. Why? Are you *still* hunting for a patch kit? I told you weeks ago to go to Pinetop-Lakeside, didn't I?"

He scrubbed a hand along his bearded jaw, a smile

tugging. "Yes, you did. But Grandma Mae sent me down here to pick up Anasazi beans for dinner tonight. Corn bread mix, too."

Even with their origins dating back to the ancient Indians of the same name, she'd never heard of that type of bean until she moved to Arizona. "Well, at least those items are something we do have in stock."

He swept off his hat and motioned her toward the entrance. "Shall we, then?"

She hesitated, then led the way into the shadowed interior of the two-story, stone-fronted building. As always, she found herself drawn to the ambiance of the beamed-ceiling space. The wooden floors. Navajo rugs adorning the walls. A lingering scent of smoke from the cast-iron woodstove.

"Is Gina still hanging on to her hat?"

Pausing at the dried goods shelf, she pulled out a bag of the sweet, nutty beans, their distinctive red-and-white markings showing clearly through the packaging. "She won't let that cap out of her sight. She even sleeps with it now."

"She can be mighty proud of the man who wore it."

Her gaze flickered to his. "Yes, she can."

Self-consciously she moved farther down the aisle and pointed to a rectangular box. "Is this the corn bread mix Mae's looking for?"

"Seeing as how it's the only brand in stock, I'm guessing it is." He reached for it with a beleaguered grunt. "If it's not, I guarantee you she'll send me right back to exchange it."

"Poor baby," she found herself saying with an almost teasing lilt as they walked side by side to the checkout counter. "But I get the impression you'd be more than happy to make another trip to the Warehouse for her, wouldn't you?"

A flash of alarm lit his gaze, then extinguished just as abruptly. What was that about?

"You're right. There's nothing on the planet I wouldn't do for that woman, that's for sure."

"Mae's fortunate to have you here," she said, ringing up the grocery items. Mae, always a cheerful sort, seemed even happier since his return. "Which reminds me, thanks for fixing the faucet and the miniblinds. I come in almost every day and feel like I'm living a fairy tale. You know, where the brownies and elves slip in overnight to do their thing?"

He squinted one eye. "I think I'm a little too big to qualify for an elf, don't you?"

She let an amused gaze rove over him, picturing him with pointy ears and boots curled up at the toes. "A supersize one maybe?"

He grinned as he paid her, then glanced almost reluctantly at his watch. "Well, I better get moving. Grandma will want to get started on dinner early so I don't miss my meeting."

"What meeting would that be?" Surely a community forum like she'd be attending wouldn't hold any appeal for him.

His forehead creased. "City council. Special assembly."

"I didn't know you took an interest in the inner workings of Canyon Springs government."

He studied her for a long moment. "There are lots of things you don't know about me, Sandi Bradshaw."

He winked, tipped his hat and headed to the door.

Whew. For a second there when she got that bright look in her eye and said she imagined he wouldn't mind another trip to the Warehouse, he thought—well, he wasn't quite sure what he thought. Except that maybe *she* thought he was making up excuses to come down there to see her.

At least things didn't seem so tense between them now. And thinking back, she didn't tell him what to do about anything, either. That was progress. Maybe they could coexist in the same town after all. He'd actually found himself relaxing in her presence, although she'd seemed surprised that he might have an interest in city government. Like that was too intellectual for him?

What she didn't know, though, was that he had a personal stake in tonight's proceedings, that he waited to hear word on that firefighting opening that had been put on hold months ago. The new budget could be a deal breaker. The fire chief was certain he'd be a shoo-in for the position, but if the funding didn't come through…

How long could he keep things together in Canyon Springs for himself and Grandma without a decent-paying job? Early on in his army career he hadn't been a diligent saver except for a sizable cut faithfully sent home to Grandma Mae. It would cost tens of thousands to remodel the lower floor of her house. To make it handicapped accessible. From what he'd seen while prowling around the place this week, it needed all new wiring and plumbing, too, not just a cosmetic makeover.

"Bryce!"

Just as he crossed Main Street, he looked up to see Joe Diaz, Meg's husband, headed in his direction. An ex-navy guy and now a regional paramedic, he and Bryce had known each other in school. While Joe had a longer history with God, he'd recently deepened that connection. So the two men were on more even ground than what Bryce felt with some other church-going guys.

"How's life, bud?" Joe thrust out his hand for a shake.

"Decent. Yourself?"

"Keeping busy. Hey, are you joining the Bible study this summer? It's just getting under way. Great opportunity to get to know some rock-solid men who'll hold you accountable. You know, Proverbs 27:17. Iron-sharpening-iron stuff."

"Not sure I'd fit in. This is all pretty new to me. My background isn't—"

"Hey, we all started right where you are."

But he had more baggage than most.

Joe adjusted the ball cap on his head. "Do what you want. But it's what I need right now. Man-to-man stuff. Keeps me moving in the right direction."

"You're married, though. Have a kid."

"So? Until last March I was single again after my

first wife died. Several years on my own. I know the challenges of single life firsthand. So give it some thought."

Bryce nodded. He could promise that much, but no more.

"Say," Joe continued, "if you don't have other plans, drop by our place tonight. Kara Dixon and Trey Kenton are coming over for dinner. Meg's whipping up a batch of my dad's homemade salsa. We'd love to have you join us."

Bryce held up his grocery bag. "Thanks, but I have supper right here, compliments of Grandma."

Joe laughed. "I can't compete with your granny's home cooking. But how about next weekend? We're getting together at Casey Lake for a barbecue with some old pals and their significant others."

"That's doable."

"Great. Saturday night. Six o'clock. Bring a date if you want to."

Bryce grimaced.

Grinning, Joe punched him playfully in the shoulder. "You don't have to. But I'm giving you warning that if you show up stag, you're fair game for my wife's matchmaking schemes and I won't be held responsible."

"Thanks for the heads-up."

"Anytime. That's what friends are for. See you then."

Bryce headed for home, his thoughts troubled. Joe's wife, Meg, was a real sweetheart. He'd worked with her on the parsonage remodel last winter, but he'd deliberately steered clear of single women the past several years. That seemed the best plan for the time being. He still had lots to figure out about how God's men were supposed to think and act. How New Bryce was expected to behave. So he sure didn't need Meg telling him what to do about his nonexistent love life.

Besides, he didn't know any single women he could ask to join him at the cookout.

Except Sandi.

And that wasn't going to happen.

"As an educator and a parent," Sandi concluded, weak-kneed as she stood before a wall-to-wall crowd in the city hall building, "I believe it's vital that the heritage of our children be supported and preserved. It's up to us to anchor them. Connect them to their roots—their inheritance. To show them that we are proud of who we are in Canyon Springs. And that they can be proud, too."

The room erupted in applause and cheers, a gavel pounding to bring the meeting back to order. A tingling sensation raced up her spine as she again found her seat, clasped her hands to still their trembling. At least she hadn't burst into tears when it was announced funding for the museum would be discontinued. Somehow she'd managed to rise to her feet when called upon to speak.

She'd agreed with the need for cutbacks and responsible spending. Had pointed out that while the amount provided for supplementing museum operations was a drop in the bucket of the city's budget deficit, it made up a significant portion of the museum's means of livelihood. She made it clear that the future of the museum during this economic downturn was in serious question—especially combined with the rent increase set to go into effect.

She'd caught Bryce's eye at that point—and his frown when others followed the trajectory of her gaze. Now she avoided looking at him, remembering how she hadn't told him she was coming to the meeting, even when he'd mentioned he intended to. Did he think she'd been deceptive? Set an ambush for him?

She shifted uncomfortably as the council spokesman moved on to the next item on the budget-balancing agenda. Library fines up by a cent. An increase in parks and rec use fees as well as on insufficient funds checks written to the city. A possible parking charge at Casey Lake. Escalating special-event liquor license rates. Installing meters along Main Street was now under consideration, as well.

With the uproar ensuing from that handful of issues, the plight of the museum was quickly forgotten. Sandi slipped from the packed room unnoticed, down the stairs and into the cool night air.

Heart pounding, she leaned back against the stone facade and closed her eyes. She'd done what she could. But it didn't look hopeful even though before the night was over there would be, as always, accusations of financial mismanagement and battle cries to "cut the fat" at the top levels of city government. Counteraccusations would follow that Canyon Springs citizens lived in a make-believe world if they thought city services came cheap.

Although it was little consolation, the museum wasn't the only victim of funding cuts. The parks and rec department was under scrutiny as were two police force and firefighter positions currently standing unfilled. The senior citizens facility, youth baseball, city pool and a dozen others were facing major cutbacks, and there had been talk of across-the-board city salary and benefits reductions. Layoffs.

"For a moment I thought I heard a fife and drum in there," a low male voice said. "Nice speech."

Startled, she bolted away from the wall and spun to face Bryce Harding, who stood but a few feet from her.

She folded her arms, endeavoring to still her racing heart. He couldn't be happy with her. Not when she practically pointed an accusing finger at him. "Do I detect a note of sarcasm?"

"None intended."

"Right." She shook her head as she fished her keys out of her jacket pocket and turned to where she'd parked her car, too weary to tangle with him tonight.

He snagged her upper arm, drawing her to a halt.

"Could we talk a minute?"

She didn't attempt to suppress a sigh. "You know how I feel about the museum and the city-funding cut.

About the rent increase. I don't know what else there is to say."

"I want you to know I wouldn't encourage Grandma to raise the rent on the museum if I had a choice."

"Oh. That's right. The trip to the Bahamas you so generously invited my mother-in-law to join you on."

"You know I was just being a smart mouth."

Why couldn't he admit he'd run through his army pay as if there was no tomorrow? That he couldn't find a steady job since his return. Was mooching off his grandma—and forcing the historical society to replenish his fun money.

"Regardless, the city council is going to do what they want to do. But I couldn't let their budget balancing at the museum's expense go by unchallenged. I had to make my voice heard. Speak up for the kids and the community."

"You did it well. But I have to admit your rah-rah-rah on behalf of the town surprises me."

"Why's that?"

"Unless my memory fails me, you weren't happy when Keith settled you in Canyon Springs. In all honesty, I didn't expect to come back and find you still here. Thought you'd have hightailed it back to Kansas City long ago."

She tensed. He remembered where she was from. Knew how she'd felt about Canyon Springs. Although her husband's forthrightness was something she'd loved about him—sometimes—why'd he have to be so candid with this man, his boyhood buddy? Bryce might not have been a stranger to Keith, but she didn't like him knowing personal things about her that she hadn't chosen to share.

She kept her tone even. "This is my home now."

"It's mine, too."

"For a long time it wasn't. It's my understanding—unless *my* memory fails me—you could hardly wait to get out of here. To join the army and leave Canyon Springs in your dust."

So there, big guy, something I know about you, too. Two can play this game, thanks to Keith.

His eyes narrowed in the dim glow of the streetlight, as if contemplating the next bombshell to drop on her. But after a long pause, his words came softly. "Whether you believe it or not, I don't like causing you distress, Sandi. Trust me, I know you've already been through enough."

She had been, hadn't she? But trust him?

Admittedly, she hadn't expected Bryce to acknowledge the hardships she'd faced the past five years, let alone the level of anxiety the museum issue caused her. As she returned his steady gaze, the anger—the tension coiled inside—slowly seeped out of her. And with a gentle nudge, her heart reluctantly opened to the recognition of a kindred spirit in Bryce. One born of a shared loss that had ripped their worlds apart.

She spoke softly. "Keith left a big hole in both our lives, didn't he?"

Bryce folded his muscled arms. Nodded. "He did at that."

"I'm sorry you lost your best friend." That had to have been hard on him. Had to still be hard. "Keith always said he was closer to you than to either of his real brothers. He cared about you, Bryce."

"I know he did."

They stood in silence, lost in their own thoughts as they listened to the raised voices echoing from an open window of the city hall chamber above—reminding her that the outcome of tonight's decision could seal the museum's fate. She should call an emergency meeting of the historical society. Brainstorm strategies, fundraisers. Prepare for the worst. She couldn't let the museum go down without a fight.

But she'd do nothing tonight.

"I need to get going. I left Gina with a babysitter." She turned away.

"May I walk you to your car?"

The earnestness in his voice halted her and she again faced him. "Thanks, but that's my car right over there."

Their eyes met again. Held.

"Then good night, Sandi."

"Good night, Bryce."

She tightened her grip on her keys and moved away, uncertain as to how to deal with seeing Bryce in a different light. With acknowledging his loss. With not yet knowing how much he knew of her last encounter with her husband.

What he thought of her. Really.

And why what he thought should matter so much to her anyway.

Chapter Nine

"I thought for sure by now you'd have Bryce Harding wrapped around your little finger. Would have wooed him with your feminine charms to call off the rent increase."

Heat flooded Sandi's face at Cate Landreth's loud remark—made in front of a Saturday-afternoon gathering of a dozen historical society members. Crowded around the museum's kitchen table, they all turned to her with renewed interest. Thank goodness Bryce's grandma rarely attended the meetings and didn't hear any of this. But she couldn't help but imagine her friend Meg would find it funny—suitable revenge for when Sandi had joined in with Cate last fall in mercilessly teasing Meg about Joe Diaz only a few days after she'd met him.

"Very funny, Cate." She managed a fairly normal-sounding laugh as she met the roomful of curious gazes. Just what she needed. Half the town watching her every move and speculating on her love life—with Bryce of all people.

"Let's deal with reality here, folks. As I said, I got a personal call early this morning from Councilman Jake Talford that the city is indeed severing our support. He assures me that when there's strong economic recovery, the council will revisit the issue. But for the time being…"

She stood, popped the lid off a red dry-erase marker and turned to the glossy whiteboard on the easel behind her. Drawing a small circle in the middle, she labeled it "museum future," then drew a dozen or so lines radiating from it.

"What's that?" an elderly man in overalls and a cowboy hat demanded. "I ain't got no time for art lessons."

"Not art lessons, Earl. We're going to brainstorm. Put our heads together and see what we can come up with to generate more income. We need to determine where we can best focus our talents and energy."

He scoffed. "I vote for you focusing your talents and energy on that Harding fellow. Less work for the rest of us."

Everyone laughed, and again a wave of warmth washed through her. She forced a laugh. "Not an option, Earl."

"Party pooper."

"Okay now, let's get started so I can keep my promise to get you out of here in an hour. So Cate, you've helped with fundraisers for years. What are a few you'd recommend?"

Basking in the spotlight, Cate sashayed around the table and took the marker from Sandi's hand. "Bake sale. Car wash. Selling candles and chocolate bars. Oh, and can't forget the popcorn. That caramel-and-peanut kind goes over big."

She printed her suggestions at the end of half a dozen spokes on the board, then sat down.

A hand raised. "At Christmas the PTA sells homemade tamales. Maybe we could make enchiladas. Have people preorder them. Or have a taco bar at the softball games."

"Navajo tacos would be even better," another chimed in, and Sandi's inner eye flew to the puffy, plate-size dough traditionally prepared over an open flame and topped with a variety of mouthwatering options. "We could do the honey-with-powdered-sugar ones. Or the beef-and-beans kind."

Sandi nodded and wrote down the ideas, relieved that the focus was off her love life. More hands shot up.

"Pancake breakfast."

"Fun run. Fish fry."

"Fajita cook-off."

"Horseshoe tournament," Earl threw in, getting into the spirit of things.

She drew more lines radiating from the circle and wrote as fast as she could. "These are great ideas, keep them coming."

Twenty minutes later the whiteboard was overflowing, words cramped into tiny print and squashed sideways into the margins. She stepped back and viewed their handiwork.

"Isn't this awesome? Great work."

A round of applause filled the little room.

She promised to transcribe the mess on the board and send it to everyone for review prior to their next meeting. With Independence Day only three weeks away, they had a lot of work ahead of them.

When the last society member departed, Sandi gathered her things, removed the whiteboard from the easel and let herself out the back door, eager to pick up Gina from Meg's. The membership had been more supportive, more enthusiastic than she'd anticipated once they'd gotten their focus off Cate and Earl's plan for her to make a pass at Bryce. Interestingly, she'd not heard a peep of outright criticism of Bryce or his grandma from the membership, so they must be buying the story that Mae was in need of additional funds. It seemed a bit too coincidental, though, that this sudden need arose with her grandson's return home.

At least none of the usual down-in-the-mouth detractors had shown up, which enabled the meeting to run more smoothly. No doubt she'd hear from them when they received the list from the brainstorming session and realized there would be work to do.

Arms full, she awkwardly locked up, trying not to smear the unwieldy dry-erase board. As she started down the back porch steps, she glimpsed Bryce and Mae approaching from the driveway. He steadied his grandmother, then loped forward to take the whiteboard from her.

"You going to the car with this?" He held it out at arm's length, as if trying to make sense of the jumbled text.

"What do you have here, dear?" Mae motioned to the board as she drew closer.

"Fundraiser ideas. The city's trimming their budget—including historical society support."

"Bryce told me. What can I do to help?"

Bryce's brows lowered as he fixed a look on Sandi that spoke volumes. *Don't even think of telling her she can ditch the rent increase.*

"We haven't decided which projects will give the greatest returns, but I'm optimistic we'll make that decision shortly. I think there will be a number of things you can assist with. We have a lot of work ahead of us."

Mae smiled at her with concern-filled eyes. "I hope you're not overdoing it at the museum this summer. I see your car out here more often than it should be. You need to take a break. Take some time for yourself."

"Fortunately, I don't require a lot of 'me' time."

"It's healthy to get out and have some fun."

"Gina and I are sleeping over at her grandma's tonight, so no cooking on my part. That's a welcome break."

"An evening with a mother-in-law isn't what I had

in mind. You need to get out with young folks. Relax and enjoy adult conversation. Bryce is going to a cookout with friends next Saturday. You should join him." She looked up at her grandson expectantly.

Sandi met his gaze with alarm. Was Mae trying to be nice—or setting them up? She hated setups. Had been dodging them for years since Keith's death. People meant well, but relationships couldn't be forced. She had to have more in common with a man than merely both being single.

He cleared his throat and his gaze flickered from his grandma to her again. "You'd be welcome to come along. They said I could bring a friend."

A friend. As in a date. No, thank you.

"Thanks for the invitation, but I have so much going on right now."

"Which is exactly why you should go." Mae patted her arm. "Your summer will be over before you know it."

It *would* be nice to get out on more than a playdate with other mothers. To think about something other than museum business. But she'd always felt guilty leaving Gina with a sitter more often than necessary.

"She's wavering, Bryce." Mae nodded at her grandson. "Convince her."

Sandi's eyes met his again, sensing his grandma was backing them both into a corner. "I appreciate the invitation, but—"

"She doesn't want to go, Grandma."

"Nonsense." Mae's chin jutted obstinately.

"Back in a minute, Gran." Bryce stepped between Sandi and his grandmother. Then motioning toward the little graveled parking lot, he herded Sandi in that direction like a cowboy rounding up strays.

Uncomfortably conscious of the big man accompanying her, she strode to her car and opened the back door so he could place the whiteboard inside.

"Sorry about that, Sandi."

She didn't have to ask what he was referring to.

"But she's right, you know." He opened the driver's-side door and she slipped into the bucket seat, then turned to look up at him. "You deserve some fun."

He glanced at the ground. Scuffed a tennis shoe-clad toe in the cinder rock. "So, you know, if you change your mind, just give me a call. Invitation still stands."

"I appreciate that. But summer's only begun and it's filled with work, friends and family." With a smile she reached for the car door handle. "And surely you haven't forgotten that this *is* a small town. I think we'd both agree showing up together would imply more things to your friends than you'd want implied."

He shrugged. "I can handle it. Never put much stock in what people have to say about me."

"Lucky you. As a widowed woman I find myself all too often the source of unwelcome speculation. I have to be constantly on my guard to protect my—"

"Reputation?"

Heat flooded her face as the insensitivity of her words belatedly struck her. As if being seen with him—a man with his sullied background—would sink her upright, pristine standing in the community.

"I didn't mean—"

"I know you didn't." He gave a self-deprecating smile and stepped back. "Have a good rest of your day, Sandi."

With a casual wave he turned away.

Mortified, she stared at his retreating back. Watched as he bent to speak to his grandma, then slipped an arm around her waist and helped her to the stairs leading to her apartment. How could she have spoken like that, so tactlessly, without even thinking how it might come across?

She momentarily squeezed her eyes shut, then pulled the car door closed and started the engine.

Please, God, forgive me. Will I never learn to think before I speak?

"I wasn't trying to set you up with her, Bryce." With an aggrieved sigh at his accusation, Grandma Mae headed to the tiny living area just off the kitchen that did double duty as Bryce's sleeping quarters. She eased down on the upholstered sofa. "I'm concerned about her."

He lowered himself into a nearby recliner, Sandi's words about guarding her reputation still stinging. In the past he'd have laughed it off. He'd never much cared what people thought about him, one way or another. Why was this any different?

Grandma straightened a plush throw pillow, then

fixed him with an accusing eye. "When are you going to tell her and the historical society about the remodeling plans?"

He scratched his bearded jawline with a knuckled hand. "No point in alarming everybody just yet. I'm checking out the home supply places to estimate the cost plus labor for anything I can't do myself. When that firefighter position opens up I won't have much free time, so likely won't be doing it all myself."

Which meant more money. But it was still cheaper than buying a new house.

Grandma reached for her crochet basket. "What happens if the job doesn't come through? Do you plan to stick around Canyon Springs and work odd jobs until you're my age?"

"We'll cross that bridge when we come to it." He gave her a confident smile, unwilling to admit the possibility had already occurred to him. Concerned him. "It'll work out. God's timing, isn't that what you always say? I'm settling into civilian life, getting reacquainted with the town. Joining up with the fire department will be like reenlisting. My time won't be my own. So this is a good break. God only knows I needed it."

Grandma pulled out her crochet hook and a skein of pumpkin-colored yarn. "You've seen a lot of things in your young life that most people hope never to see."

He nodded, memory flickering to the heat. The cold. The grittiness. The odors. The fear. Death. He plucked at the fabric on the arm of his chair. "I know

Grandpa did a stint in the army, but why'd you let me join, Gran? Even encouraged it."

"I thought you'd have figured that out by now."

"It was because of Jenn, wasn't it?" He never called his mother by anything but her given name. "I was letting her turn me into an angry young man on a fast journey to nowhere."

"You were at that."

He rubbed his thumb along an upholstery welt. He didn't like thinking about his mother. Talking about her. "Have you heard from her lately?"

"Postcard from L.A. in April."

"She's still messed up, isn't she?"

"Drugs change a person."

And bad company corrupts. The combination was as destructive as war. "Are you ever mad at God, Grandma? That he let this happen to her? To us?"

Goodness knows his grandparents had done their best. Grandpa had discovered Canyon Springs on an elk hunting trip and talked Grandma into resettling here, far away from the temptations of city life in Cleveland, Ohio. Jenn was fourteen then and already heading down the wrong path.

A change of scenery didn't do one lick of good.

Grandma shook her head, concentrating on securing the crochet hook in her gnarled fingers. "Jenn made bad choices despite her upbringing. Continues to make them. Being mad at God is a waste of time, don't you think? He's our only hope that someday her eyes will be opened before it's too late."

She shifted to a more comfortable position, her keen gaze now fixed on him. "What about you? Are you mad at God because of her? Because you don't know who your father is? I honestly don't think she knows, Bryce. I believe with all my heart that she'd tell you if she knew."

His jaw tightened. "Probably better not to know and risk hating him."

"Like you hate your mother?"

"I don't hate her, Gran." But he had for a lot of years—or had tried to. Until God got hold of him.

Grandma set her crochet work aside, her eyes filled with love and concern. "I've long feared Jenn's over-bearing, unreliable disposition may have colored your perceptions of women. That that's why you've never found one to commit to."

His mind flashed to Sandi and the unreasonable demands she'd put on Keith. Do this. Don't do that. Sit. Speak. Shake. Roll over.

In spite of himself, he smiled and settled more deeply into the recliner, forcing himself to relax. "I can't say that I'm not overly sensitive to, shall we say, women with dictatorial inclinations."

A knowing look glistened in Grandma Mae's eyes. "You know God's going to send you a strong-willed woman to partner with for a lifetime, don't you? One who'll challenge you, keep you on your toes. Who won't let you get away with anything. Mark my words, that's the kind of woman that will make you happiest."

"When pigs fly."

"You'd be miserable with a whatever-you-say-sir gal."

"I'm actually thinking I might hunt me up one of those meet-me-at-the-door-with-a-kiss-and-my-house-slippers models."

And why was it Sandi's face, of all people, that came to mind when he envisioned such a greeting? Imagined a kiss that would send the memories of the day's trials and tribulations scurrying for the hills.

But Sandi "Bossy Boots" Bradshaw? She'd likely tell him to fetch his own slippers and, while he was at it, take out the garbage, mow the lawn and get the laundry started.

No thanks.

Grandma reached again for her crochet hook. "You'd be bored to tears with a follow-your-orders kind of wife."

He banished the mental image of the too-appealing Sandi as the sting of her words about protecting her reputation—from him—stabbed afresh. "Don't count on it, Gran."

He glanced at his watch, then rose from the chair. He'd better get his Big Elf self downstairs and fix the creaking floorboard—before that little red notebook and its infamous checklist put in another appearance.

Chapter Ten

Pre-dawn light crept across the floor and illuminated the walls of Sandi's bedroom, the sheer window curtains stirring lightly in the faintest of breezes. Where had the weekend gone? And why was she lying here on a Monday thinking about Bryce Harding?

Unstructured time, such as these early morning summer hours before she threw off the covers and her feet hit the floor, had invariably drawn memories of Keith.

But this morning Bryce filled her thoughts. Did he think she'd turned down his invitation to the cookout because of his reputation as a party animal who indulged in superficial relationships? She hadn't given any thought to that at the time she'd opened her big fat mouth. She'd only been concerned with letting him off the hook after his grandma badgered him into asking her out. With letting him know that she understood he wouldn't want to appear to his old buddies or eligible females that he'd "hooked up" with her.

But two days later here she was still miserable at the misunderstanding. Keith had long prayed for Bryce—and she'd failed her husband yet again when she'd all but slammed the door in his friend's face. Unintentionally for certain, but what would be the point of trying to apologize again? Trying to explain would only be awkward for her and embarrassing for Bryce.

But should she accept his invitation after all? It wouldn't be a date exactly. Just hanging out. An opportunity to talk to him about rethinking the museum rent. An opportunity to make it up to him—and Keith—for her insensitive blunder of the other day.

"Mommy!" The whisper came accompanied by a timid knock at her closed door. "Are you awake?"

She sat up in bed and propped pillows behind her. "Good morning, Gina."

The door opened a crack and her daughter's smiling face peeped in. Then the door flung open and, with a flying leap, Gina landed on the bed and clambered into her arms.

"What are you doing up so early, sweetie?"

"You said we'd go to the park today."

"You're *sure* you still want to do that?" she teased, giving her daughter a hug.

"Yeah. Can Davy come, too?"

"I don't know. We can ask."

"I'll call him." Gina scrambled off the bed, but Sandi caught the tail of her pajama top.

"Hold on. It's only six o'clock. Too early to call. He's probably still asleep."

Gina collapsed again on the bed. "We could wake him up."

"I don't think his mom and dad would appreciate that."

"Maybe Uncle Bryce can come. I bet he's awake."

Uncle Bryce. Gina had "slipped" again on Saturday night when relating to her grandma how a few weeks earlier he'd put her in his boat and let her pretend to row. That faux pas had earned Sandi a disapproving look from LeAnne.

"If he's awake it's because he has to go to work." Wherever that happened to be.

"Or fishing."

"Right. So why don't you scoot off to get dressed. Play while I shower. Then we'll have breakfast, drop some things off at the post office and hit the park."

By seven-thirty they were there, joined by other early bird moms and kids determined to beat the heat. While this time of year it was still fairly cool overnight, afternoons during the weeks before the summer monsoons swept in sent temperatures rising into the upper eighties and even nineties. Not that the heat here, with its low humidity, was like anything she'd experienced growing up in Missouri.

Last night she'd emailed the historical society members a list of suggested fundraising projects, then today had snail-mailed those who didn't have internet connections. *Please, Lord, let them all come to a consensus.* She had her own preferences—ones that would take the least ramp-up time and produce results most quickly. With Independence Day just around the corner, that would be a peak time to pick the pockets, so to speak, of summer visitors. Too many Canyon Springs fundraisers depended on the generosity of locals repeatedly dipping into shallow pocketbooks and wallets throughout the other nine months of the year.

"Sandi!"

She looked up from pushing Gina on the swing to see historical society member Sharlene Odel striding across the grass toward her, her little leashed Pekingese, Buffy, waddling breathlessly beside her. Sharlene, a former president of the organization, was now one of those rarely active members who stepped in only when something displeased her.

Bending to pick up her daughter's favorite cap where it had been placed out of harm's way, she allowed Gina to pump on her own and moved some distance from the swings to meet her sometimes adversary. Pasted on a smile. "Good morning, Shar."

"If you say so." The forty-something woman tossed back her French-braided, bleached-blond hair with an impatient movement. An attractive woman—or she would be if she'd do away with the perpetual crease of disapproval in her brow. "I got your email last night. So what's this fundraising business all about? When I turned the society presidency over to you two years ago, our finances were as healthy as can be. Robust. I can only assume that the current board is mishandling the monies."

Leave it to Shar to get to the heart of things.

"Then you'd assume wrong." Sandi put a teasing lilt into her tone, hoping to drown out the growl that threatened to rumble from her throat. "As has been indicated in our quarterly newsletters over the past two years, the drop in summer visitors has taken its toll on our bank account. And with a property-rent increase on the horizon and the city council cutting funds, it's time to replenish our bank account."

"There should have been enough set back to tide us over this rough spot."

"I can assure you, there wasn't."

Sharlene jerked roughly on a wandering-off Buffy's leash, sending the pudgy little canine into a rollover. "Before we launch into any of these major projects, I'm going to recommend to the membership that we have the books audited by an unbiased outside source. My cousin, Andy, is a bookkeeper at—"

"If you'll recall," Sandi interrupted before she had to endure a rundown of cousin Andy's resumé, "we had an independent auditor in last winter. The books were spotless. We received accolades for funds management in a severe economic downturn."

Shar waved her away. "Well, I don't have time to stand here and argue with you. But you'll be hearing from me again. Soon. No offense, you understand, but it wasn't farsighted of the membership to vote an outsider into office."

She snatched a squirming Buffy into her arms and strode away, not waiting for a response.

Sandi stared after her. *Outsider.* Even with seven years of throwing herself into endless community volunteer work, she remained an interloper to some. She'd done everything she could to endear herself to the historical society's membership. To convince them she was as much a part of Canyon Springs as any of the old-timers. Hoping, praying, it would be a natural progression for the members to dedicate the new space in her husband's memory.

But it was obvious she wouldn't be getting Sharlene's support.

With a sigh, she turned again toward Gina just as a bicyclist cruised to an abrupt halt but a few feet from her.

"What was that all about?" Gripping the handlebars, Bryce anchored his bike between his legs and nodded toward Sharlene's retreating back. He hadn't intended to stop, but when he'd seen that Pekingese-packing woman's hands go to her hips and her head start wagging in that condescending way she had about her, he couldn't sail on by.

Sandi's stiff smile relaxed. "Another satisfied historical society customer. I think she's going to push for impeachment of its president."

"Grandma says Shar's nothing but a hardheaded know-it-all." He rapped knuckles on the side of his biking helmet to illustrate.

She laughed. "Have to say I agree, but if you repeat that to anyone I'll deny it."

Sandi sure looked pretty this morning in that lacy tank top and shorts, her dainty feet slipped into sparkly sandals.

"Your secret's safe with me." He pulled off his helmet, looped the chin strap over the handlebars and ruffed up his hair with a bike-gloved hand. Then he glanced toward the swings where Gina was pumping herself ever higher, her squeals ringing out in the clear morning air. "Out early to dodge the heat, huh?"

"You bet." She glanced toward Gina, then back at him, her gaze uncertain.

"Something wrong?"

She compressed her lips as if deciding how to respond, then took a quick breath. "I've been thinking about what your grandma said. About getting out more. About going to the cookout with your friends."

His heart jerked at the unexpected direction the conversation was taking. Tamped down the outlandish hope that her words elicited. What was with him? She'd been right to turn him down to begin with. A "good girl" seen hanging out with him wasn't the wisest move. He'd already had old acquaintances punching him playfully in the arm and commenting on his being seen at the equine center's grand opening with "that hot widow."

Sure, he'd turned over a new leaf, gotten his heart scrubbed squeaky clean, but it could be a long time before his reputation followed suit. If ever. The past tagged along behind him, a perpetual cloud of trailing dust like with Charlie Brown's friend Pigpen.

"If the invitation is still open," she ventured, fiddling with the army cap in her hands, "I'd like to go."

He heard the words, but the uncertainty in her eyes gave away that she wasn't confident in what she was saying. Why'd she change her mind about going with him anyway? But if he didn't assure her the invitation still stood, she'd think he held a grudge about the earlier put-down.

He cleared his throat and tightened his fingers on the bicycle handlebars. "Sure, it's still open."

Was that disappointment clouding her eyes? Like maybe she'd hoped for an excuse not to go?

"Great. You said Saturday night? Where and what time? I can meet you there."

Talk about making it clear she was a free, independent agent. Making sure he didn't misconstrue the outing as a date. Well, that was fine with him. Dating Keith's wife was the furthest thing from *his* mind.

"Six o'clock. Casey Lake. Bristlecone ramada."

She nodded. "I know where that is. What's on the menu? I can bring a side dish."

He hadn't asked about the food. Probably should check with Joe about what he should bring, too. "Burgers, most likely. About anything goes with that."

"Maybe cheesy potatoes then—a baked hash browns dish with cheddar cheese and onion. Does that sound good?"

"Yeah, sure." Fried grasshoppers sounded good to him at the moment. He hadn't had breakfast yet.

"Uncle Bryce! Uncle Bryce!" Out of nowhere a

flying weight plowed into him as Gina threw her arms around one of his legs. He braced himself to keep the bicycle from toppling them, then reached down and swept her into his arms.

"Hey, kid."

She patted him on the shoulder. "Did you see me swinging?"

"Sure did. How'd you go so high?"

"Mommy taught me."

He glanced at Sandi. "Is that a fact."

But the child's mother was scanning the other park-goers, most likely wondering who'd heard the Uncle Bryce thing. But then, apparently satisfied, she turned back to him with a laugh. With an unexpected jolt, he glimpsed the dimpled, beaming six-year-old she'd once been, flying to the sky in her swing. Blond hair streaming out behind her, glinting in the sun.

She folded her arms with sassy bravado. "Nobody outswings the Bradshaw women, right Gina?"

Gina nodded with enthusiasm, looping her arm around Bryce's neck. "The Bradshaw women are the best, right, Uncle Bryce?"

He gave her a squeeze, but his eyes were drawn again to her pretty mother. He winked. "You bet."

Color rose in Sandi's cheeks. What had gotten into him this morning? Flirting with Keith's wife. Just because she'd decided—for whatever reason—to go on the outing, that didn't mean she was looking for anything else from him. And he sure didn't want anything else from her, either.

She held out Keith's cap to her daughter. "Say good-bye and hop on down, Gina. We have a lot to do this morning and I'm sure we've delayed Bryce from his morning cycling much too long."

He returned Gina's hug and set her back on the ground. She plopped the cap on her head with a cocky grin that mirrored her daddy's, and he watched as the pair strolled away, hand in hand to their car. Gina chattered the whole while, skipping along with energy to burn.

Cute kid. Made him smile.

And then there was her mother...

An unexpected sense of anticipation rose up in him. Less than a week and she'd meet him at the lake. Even if it wasn't technically a date—she'd made that clear—they'd probably hang out together, wouldn't they? Joe and Meg were married. Jason and Reyna, too. Trey and Kara were as good as hitched.

He slipped his helmet on again, watching as Sandi's car pulled away.

Keith would be proud of both his girls. Hard to understand, though, why his buddy had been taken to his heavenly home when he'd still had so much to live for. And why God left some no-good fella like himself on the planet instead.

What would Keith think about Sandi joining his best friend at a barbecue? He certainly wouldn't have approved of Old Bryce going anywhere near her, that was for sure.

But what about New Bryce?

And would inviting Sandi along get him off the matchmaking hook with Meg?

Or make things worse?

"Don't worry about tomorrow," he'd read in the Good Book that very morning. "Today has enough trouble of its own."

And that was supposed to be reassuring?

He let out a huff of pent-up breath and launched off on his bike.

Chapter Eleven

Already Thursday afternoon and she'd been so flustered with this whole barbecue thing that Sandi had forgotten to get a babysitter for Saturday night. She'd been so intent on what she'd say and how she'd say it to get Bryce to rethink the museum increase that she'd fumbled a critical aspect of the entire evening. Unfortunately, if she recalled correctly, Joe Diaz didn't have to work this weekend, so Meg wasn't an option. They'd want family time. Sharon Dixon would be out of town.

Cassidy Donne. That was it. One of her students. She'd announced on the last day of school that she was saving for a trip to England so she planned to babysit her heart out this summer. Perfect.

But during her first break between a steady stream of Warehouse customers, a call to her student proved futile. Cassidy suggested a couple of friends, but they, too, were booked Saturday night.

Well, she'd think of something. LeAnne maybe?

She'd volunteered to keep Gina for the entire summer, but sentencing the active little girl to long afternoons with her grandma hadn't seemed the wisest alternative. And if she asked LeAnne to babysit, wouldn't she want to know why? Not a good idea.

She glanced around the Warehouse's spacious interior, making sure no customers required her attention, then focused on tidying up at the front counter. Even now, days since her encounter with Bryce in the park, she didn't know why she'd committed herself to accompanying him. Well, not accompanying him exactly. She'd told him she'd meet him there.

She cringed. Was that rude? She was so out of practice with dating etiquette, having not been on one—except with Keith—since he'd responded to her letter while she was in college. But then this wasn't really a date. Meeting Bryce left them both with open options to come and go as they pleased. If there was a woman among his friends who liked him or whom he liked, it wouldn't be as if they'd shown up together. Or giving the impression that they were a couple.

What an idiot she was to have pushed Bryce into this.

Then another thought struck her. What would she wear to meet his friends? Jeans? Shorts? A sundress? She didn't have anything new. She'd been scrimping and saving every dime from her Warehouse job the past several years to buy museum display cases. Maybe she and Gina could run over to Show Low, check out the shops. But would something that looked new imply to others—to Bryce—that this *was* a date?

The same overactive butterflies that had assaulted the insides of her stomach since Monday morning renewed their battering-ram efforts.

"Good afternoon, Sandi."

Startled, she swung to face her mother-in-law. Guilty warmth crept up her neck. She had a not-a-date with a man LeAnne despised.

"Hi. What brings you in today?"

"I dropped off a pair of slacks at the dry cleaner and thought I'd pop in to see if you were working this afternoon."

"Yep, I'm here."

"And while I'm here I may as well let you know—a dear friend of mine called this morning. She's coming up from the Valley tomorrow to pick up a rocking chair I found for her at that antique shop down the street. She'll head home Saturday morning, but that conflicts with our Friday get-together. So let's shift our time to Saturday."

A free Friday night? Her heart lightened, but only momentarily. "This Saturday?"

"That's not convenient?"

Steady, girl. Keep it vague. "I'm getting together with friends."

"Oh?"

She sounded as if she was surprised Sandi had any. "Friends of friends, actually. A cookout at Casey Lake."

"And Gina's going, too?"

"Actually, no. It's an adult gathering." She took a deep breath. "Did you want to babysit?"

There, she'd asked her.

LeAnne's expression warmed. "You know I'm always more than happy to spend time with my granddaughter."

"Gina enjoys her time with you, too."

Usually.

"So who are these friends of friends? Like a church group?"

LeAnne *would* have to ask. She herself hadn't asked Bryce that question because she didn't want him to take it as rudeness on her part, as if checking them out for suitability after she'd made that blunder involving concern for her reputation.

To Sandi's relief, a customer approached. With seeming reluctance, LeAnne moved away to peruse a rack of postcards. With any luck, the break in conversation would be a sufficient distraction to get her off the topic she'd honed in on as if sensing her daughter-in-law was hiding something.

Which she was. Sort of.

Sandi took her time ringing up the armload of outdoor gear, chatting with the customer, recommending camping sites as if she were an outdoor pro. In reality, she'd camped only once in her life. With Keith. It had been a disaster. But she'd all but memorized the chamber of commerce guide so she could intelligently advise visitors on the community's many opportunities for outdoor recreation.

All the while, though, she kept a furtive eye on her mother-in-law, hoping she'd grow impatient with the chitchat and scurry off to the next event in her always busy schedule. But the moment the satisfied customer headed to the shop door, LeAnne returned to the counter, her manicured hand resting on the polished surface. Click. Click. Click.

"So who is this friend who has these friends?"

Think fast. "Mae Harding—who lives above the museum—suggested I go. She thinks I need to get out more often with adults my age."

"Like with her grandson?" LeAnne's voice came low and sharp, her gaze piercing.

Sandi lowered her own voice. "I'm meeting him and some of his friends at the lake. It's not a date or anything even remotely close to one."

"*His* friends? My land, Sandi, what are you thinking? Have you no concept of how quickly an attractive young woman can shred a spotless reputation in this town? I can't believe you'd be so careless with your—and Keith's—hard-earned standing in the community. With little Gina's."

"There's no reason for concern. I'll be in a public place in broad daylight." Then again, who *were* Bryce's friends? It hadn't dawned on her that his local chums might be every bit as rowdy as those he associated with while in the military.

"Reconsider, Sandi. This is foolishness."

"I already agreed to go." She'd turned him down

once. She couldn't do it again. Besides, the museum's future was at stake.

LeAnne braced herself on the checkout counter. "Sweetheart, I understand that as a single parent you feel isolated from your peers. Feel the weight of responsibility on your young shoulders. Feel as if the world is passing you by while everyone else is having a good time. But that's the price you sometimes have to pay. For the sake of your husband's memory. Your daughter's future."

"I'm sure it will be okay. I don't see any way to get out of it now."

"You pick up the phone and—" LeAnne's lips tightened. Then she stepped back from the counter. "I can't be a party to this and babysit Gina for you. So count me out of the equation."

Raising a disapproving brow at Sandi, she strode briskly out the door.

Was LeAnne right? What if the gathering turned out to be like one of those off-campus picnics in college that deteriorated as the sun set. What if she found herself surrounded by drinking. Drugs. Even if she left immediately, what might the outcome be if she were thought to be a part of that?

Surely Bryce wouldn't invite her to something of that nature, would he? But was she willing to risk losing her hard-earned relationship with Keith's beloved mom just to prove a point?

She took a ragged breath. She owed Keith so much. Had no other choice. She'd have to beg off.

* * *

Thursday night Bryce hung up the phone on his grandma's kitchen wall and ran a hand through his still shower-damp hair.

If that didn't beat all. Sandi had turned him down. Again. Twice for the same event. If this kept up, he'd develop some kind of inferiority complex. From the time he'd started going out in high school, he'd never been turned down for a date.

Not that this was a date.

Nevertheless, the rejection stung.

"She dumped you?"

Not having his cell phone number, Sandi had called the house, so the entire minute-and-a-half conversation played out to the eavesdropping ears of his granny. He again ran his hand through his hair.

"You could see for yourself, right at the beginning, that she wasn't jumping up and down with excitement when I asked her to go with me."

"That's because of the way you asked. Like somebody'd put a gun to your head to get the words out of your mouth."

He gave her a significant look. "I think it was pretty clear to both Sandi and me who was holding that gun."

Sandi had been apologetic enough in their brief phone conversation. But she sounded nervous. Almost as if afraid he'd challenge her for an explanation that was more explicit than the vague one she offered. He didn't challenge her, though. He was smart enough to recognize a brush-off.

"Maybe something *did* come up," Grandma assured. "Something legitimate."

He shrugged.

But Grandma could be right. Sandi wanted only to *meet* him at the lake, didn't she? Maybe because there was some other guy she was sweet on. She didn't want to be seen with Keith's old buddy and scare the other dude off. Maybe she'd gotten a genuine date for Saturday night?

He mulled that revelation for a moment, rolling it around in his mind. Who? That new city councilman, Jake Talford? Maybe that new guy who'd shown up at church last week?

Not that it was any of his business, but in Keith's absence, he couldn't help but feel protective of Sandi. Lots of jerks out there looking to take advantage of nice women. He himself might not have settled down with any of his lady friends from the past, but he sure had done his best not to be a jerk. But if any unsavory sort hooked up with Sandi Bradshaw, they might get a rude awakening when she pulled out that little red notebook of hers and outlined the direction their life would take henceforth. All the way to the grave.

"Why are you grinning?" Grandma Mae placed her hands on her hips, eyes sharp. "You seem pretty tickled for a man who just got turned down."

He shook his head, but couldn't suppress the smile. The thought of some unsuspecting male getting ambushed by Widow Bradshaw was worth smiling about. But no, he wasn't tickled at a turndown. He'd been looking forward to spending an evening with her. Would have been better than showing up stag, that's for sure. Now he'd be a sitting duck for Matchmaker Meg.

"Well, I hope this makes you smile, as well." Grandma waved a slip of paper. "I took the message while you were showering. Don't know why he didn't call your cell."

She handed him a name and phone number jotted down in her familiar script.

Brenden Gerrard. The fire chief.

This could be the make-it-or-break-it call.

Chapter Twelve

❧

"So are we all in agreement then?" Sandi stood in front of the historical society members gathered in the museum kitchen Monday night. "It's short notice to pull off something like this with the Fourth almost on top of us."

"We can do it," Earl assured, as if he'd be the one racing to get the appropriate permits, cleaning out the society's makeshift vending trailer, shopping for the best deal on ingredients—and sweating over hot grills to produce enough Navajo fry bread to keep equine center event-goers satisfied.

She owed Trey Kenton big-time for letting them slip in at the midnight hour to open a concession outside the arena. He'd even donated a side of beef for the flavorful, oversize tacos that were a regional favorite. Due to a major remodeling glitch, the venue for a three-day Fourth of July horse show scheduled in air-conditioned comfort in the Valley of the Sun had been shifted to Canyon Springs. The show sponsors sought, and found, just what they were looking for in the High Country Equine Center, and Trey hoped they'd prefer the new site in the future, as well.

"In my opinion," Sharlene Odel said, rising to her feet as she raised her voice above the excited chatter of the society members, "we wouldn't be in this predicament if the board had been taking care of business all along."

The chatter stilled. All eyes turned to Sharlene.

Then Sandi.

She'd been expecting something like this. No doubt Sharlene sensed an opportunity to drive a wedge into the for-the-most-part supportive camaraderie of the society. The seldom-seen Fran had shown up today, too. And Dana.

Coincidence? Not likely.

With a silent prayer she turned to Sharlene.

"Shar has a very good point. It's imperative that all our members take an interest in the financial health of our organization, not just relying on the elected board to carry the entire burden."

She nodded toward the society's treasurer. "Becky Ortiz is distributing printouts of our income and expenditures over the last two years. Last winter's audit report, as well. I encourage all of you to examine them at your leisure and provide feedback on how we can better manage our resources."

Sharlene, minus her Pekingese today, flashed Dana and Fran a disgruntled look. She snagged one of the sheets from Becky and held it up. "This is all nice and good. But legitimate concerns can still be raised as to the quality of a leadership that permitted our finances to fall into such a dismal state."

Cate Landreth stood, hackles almost visibly rising. Cate wasn't afraid of anyone, not even a well-entrenched member of Canyon Springs society. "No one could have anticipated the economic downturn, the subsequent need for Mae Harding to increase the museum rent or that the city would cut our funding."

"Nevertheless," Shar persisted, "with upcoming elections in September, I appeal to the membership to remember where we were two years ago when we elected the current board—and where we find ourselves today."

"Maybe if you'd have bothered to come to a meeting occasionally, Shar," Earl voiced in a lazy drawl, "you could have put that twenty-twenty hindsight of yours to good use and saved us from ourselves."

Heads nodded around the room in agreement. Voices whispered support.

Sharlene looked down a haughty nose at the impertinent speaker, no doubt preparing to put him in his place, but Sandi stepped in before things could escalate further.

"Before feelings get hurt or words are said that we might regret—" she knew all about that "—let's focus on our fundraising plans. Regardless of how we got here, we need this event to be a success."

She couldn't wrap things up and get out of there fast enough. Sharlene and her two supporters departed first, and Sandi hurried the others out behind them, insisting she couldn't linger for small talk, but needed to be on her way to pick up Gina. She didn't want to get sucked into dissing Sharlene or risk further splitting the association into factions with members feeling they needed to take sides.

When the last car pulled out, she locked up and stepped out into the darkness of the front porch. One more thing to add to her checklist—have Bryce replace that burned-out bulb. But at least she'd gotten through the evening without bloodshed.

Thank You, Lord.

"Good evening, Sandi."

Her heart shot up to her throat and it was all she could do not to stagger back from the shadowed corner from where the voice had come. She took a deep breath as recognition dawned.

Bryce.

"You scared me."

"Sorry. Didn't mean to." He rose from where he'd been seated on one of the wooden benches, obscured by the shadow of a large pine blocking the streetlight, and stepped into the slightly more illuminated portion of the porch next to her.

"What are you doing out here?" Her heart continued pounding an erratic beat.

"I'm just kickin' back, enjoying the night. Town settles down after dark. Good time to come out and take pleasure in God's handiwork. Count my blessings."

That sure didn't sound like the man her husband used to tell her about.

"I see." Acutely aware of his too-close proximity, her words sounded almost breathless even to her own ears. She took a step back. "Well, don't let me interrupt you. I'm sure living in the tiny apartment up there, you don't get a lot of privacy."

He chuckled, a low, appealing sound that caressed her ears. Made her, against her will, long to draw closer.

"That's a fact. But I don't feel the confinement so much in the summer months when I can spend a good deal of time outdoors." He chuckled again, studying her face in the dim light. It warmed under his probing eyes. He took a deep breath, his broad chest rising and falling. Such a big man. Strong. Reassuring. "So, how's museum business going? Saw tonight's crowd leave. Sharlene still leading a lynch mob?"

She gave herself a mental shake, drawing her wandering thoughts back to the conversation. "Cate Landreth backed her down tonight and I threw myself into the fray before fists started flying. I'm sure we haven't heard the last of her, but for the time being we're moving forward."

"I sure am sorry she's giving you a hard time. Grandma Mae says you've been devoted to the museum ever since Keith's passing. Have really kept it going."

"I've tried anyway." She shifted restlessly. "So how was the cookout?"

Ugh. Why'd she pick that topic? Reminding him of her rude about-face.

"Had a great time. Good food and good company. Kara's sure sweet on that Kenton fellow. I could tell something was going on between those two even early last winter. And Meg and Joe—"

"Diaz?"

"Yeah, Diaz. Several of their friends, including a few I knew from my growing-up years. The pastor and his wife, too."

Inwardly she groaned. The preacher and his wife? And she'd let her mother-in-law fill her with ridiculous, unfounded fears that sent her into a tailspin.

"I know I said it before, Bryce, but I'm really sorry for backing out on you at the last minute."

He didn't know the half of it.

He raised a halting hand. "No explanations needed."

"I'd fully intended to go, but then—" There was no point in trying to explain. What could she say? *My mother-in-law can't stand you and I'm incapable of making my own decisions?* "But thanks for the invitation."

"Some other time, maybe." He folded his arms across his chest, a smile widening. "I was on my best behavior Saturday night, so I think they'll invite me again."

"Interesting how you and Joe left town for the military, saw the wonders of the world, and still came back here."

"And you're thinking to yourself, 'Self, Joe was a

navy corpsman and now he's a paramedic, a shining example to all. Bryce on the other hand, is shoveling manure, building fences and camping out with his poor old granny.'"

That's exactly what she'd been thinking. Thank goodness in the dim light her blush wouldn't betray her. "To each his own."

He leaned in closer and her heart skittered.

"Just to set your mind at ease, Sandi, I'm caught between a rock and a hard place with the city's budget-balancing quandary. I need to be here in town for Grandma—so she doesn't have to pull up roots and move back to her no-good family in Ohio. But as you heard at the council meeting, several job openings are on hold indefinitely."

So that was what he was doing, killing time until a position opened up? That's why he needed additional income from the museum in the interim? She racked her brain for what was said at the council meeting. "The police department? Fire?"

"Firefighter," he said with evident satisfaction. "I'd done some of that when I first joined the army. Thought I'd found my calling. Then gradually those roles were phased out for the most part, contracted out. But I'd kept it in mind for once I left the service, if they'd still take an old guy like me."

"I had no idea."

"Yeah, well, now you know. But keep it to yourself, will you? The fire chief assured me again that the position's mine if he has anything to say about it.

He's negotiating with the city for funding. It's looking good. But I don't want to go around town acting like I'm a shoo-in."

"I won't say a word." But why was he telling her this at all? As if what she thought of him held some importance. Was it because he still thought she'd turned down his invitation for fear of soiling her reputation? Hadn't wanted to be seen with him where they might be mistaken as a couple? "That was a big sacrifice to quit the army to come back here for your grandma."

"I still relive the nightmare of that call rousting me out of my sleep half a world away. It's been hard to face the fact she isn't as invincible as I believed her to be as a kid."

"But you haven't been a kid for a long time, have you?"

"I guess not."

"She's lucky to have you."

"And I her. I'd been entertaining doubts of reenlisting anyway and that call sealed the deal." A faint smile touched his lips. "She pitched a fit when she found out, but by then it was too late to stop me. When she was finally released from the Pine Country Care facility, I was waiting for her."

"You considered leaving the army before Mae's injury? You were in for—what?—fifteen years?"

His open expression closed down as if realizing he'd shared too much. For a flashing second she pictured him as he'd been as a kid. Mr. Tough Guy. Armor in place. Strong jaw jutting, determined not to let the world see where it hurt.

But it did.

She could see that much—and her heart went out to the little boy he'd been. The man he was.

Even in the dim light he must have read something in her eyes for he stepped back. Rubbing the palm of his hand along his bearded jawline, he glanced in the direction of the front door. "I suppose you're adding that burned-out lightbulb to my 'to do' list?"

"Of course."

"That's what I figured."

Bryce slammed the posthole digger into the hard-packed soil with all his might. Winced when it slammed into another buried bowling ball-size rock, sending a jarring wave of painful sensation up his arms and into his shoulders.

He muttered under his breath, knowing it wasn't the rock-hard earth that troubled him, but the big, beautiful eyes of Sandi Bradshaw looking at him as if she could see straight into his soul. Under her gentle prodding, he'd been a regular windbag the other night. Mr. Macho Firefighter, making sure she knew he wasn't the loser he suspected she thought he was. For whatever reason, wanting to ensure she knew he was every bit as worthy of her attention as that other guy, whoever he was. The one who got her to back out of going to the cookout at Casey Lake.

But then she had to go and ask why he'd wanted

to leave the service. Had he confessed, the truth of it would leave him less than heroic in her eyes. No woman wanted to hear a man say fear had taken hold of him. Fear that he was burning out. Was going numb inside. That he'd so skillfully, determinedly, built walls around his mind and his heart to block the realities of his past, of war, that feeling nothing had become a desirable norm.

Stepping back to view his morning's labor, he pulled out a handkerchief, tipped back his hat and wiped his brow. Trey said he'd rent one of those powered posthole diggers for him, but Bryce wanted no part of that. He needed to stay in shape if he expected to pass the physical part of the firefighting requirements. He wasn't much of a gym club kind of guy. Manual labor suited him just fine.

Or it did most of the time.

He looked up at the sound of a truck pulling up alongside the acreage under the shade of one of the towering pines. Joe Diaz cut the engine and rolled down the window on the passenger side. Hollered out the window.

"How's it going? Looks like hot work."

Bryce rested his forearms atop the posthole digger handles. "It is at that."

"Hey, in case you're interested, the men's group is meeting tonight. Seven o'clock, my place. Meg's fixing Sharon Dixon's blue-ribbon-winning apple pie for us. You're welcome to come."

Bryce gave his forehead another swipe, then stuffed

the handkerchief in his back pocket. Adjusted his hat and sauntered over to the truck. "I'm going through that workbook you're using for the study. Doin' okay until I hit that submission stuff. Don't get me wrong, we're both military men, so we understand the concept of submitting to authority, to God. But can you tell me, Joe—what's up with this mutual submission stuff? I mean, you let Meg boss you around?"

Joe didn't laugh outright, but Bryce didn't miss the suppressed smile.

"Mutual submission isn't about bossing, Bryce, it's about respecting another person's opinions. Allowing them to have a voice, make choices and take the lead on things where God's gifted them to be the better decision maker. It's about not always having your own way."

Bryce leaned his forearms on the lower window rim of the passenger-side window. "I thought the man was supposed to take the lead. You know, head of the household."

"That's true. And way too many men abdicate their responsibilities, forcing women to step in and take over the husband's role so the home will run smoothly—then the men complain about it. But a man's also supposed to love his wife as Christ loves the church—pretty tall order—and the Bible's real clear that submission to a spouse isn't just the woman's role."

Bryce grimaced and rubbed the back of his neck. "This stuff isn't easy, is it?"

Joe did laugh at that.

"No, sometimes it's not. But I'm learning a lot from listening to the older guys in our men's group. Guys who've been happily married ten, twenty, fifty years even. You should come."

"Like I said before, I'm a newbie at all this. And I'm not married, so that makes me an odd duck at my age."

"Would you be more comfortable meeting one-on-one? Just the two of us over lunch? Or after dinner one night each week?"

Bryce shifted his weight, mulling over the proposition. "You'd be willing to do that?"

"A guy in the navy did that for me. From what you've told me, sounds like you had someone investing time in you while in the service, too."

"Yeah, Keith Bradshaw, Sandi's husband, to begin with. He laid the groundwork even though I didn't know it at the time. Then a few years after Keith's death, when I was searching for answers in earnest, another army guy and I started meeting together before he shipped out for home."

"Just say the word."

"Sounds like an offer I can't refuse." Bryce thrust his hand into the interior of the truck and the two men shook.

As Joe drove off, Bryce unsnapped the steel water bottle he'd strapped to his belt and took a long, slow drink.

Letting a girl boss you around?

I don't know about this, Lord.

Is that why Keith let Sandi call the shots sometimes? Why he'd step back and let her have her way without argument on occasion? Kept his sense of humor about it? Even the very last time he'd seen his buddy, he'd been gleefully planning and plotting how to woo Sandi to his way of thinking about something she'd drawn a line in the sand over.

But he never got a chance.

His helicopter had crashed.

Recapping the water bottle, he clipped it again to his belt. Then he ambled out to dig more postholes, trying to decide when would be the best time to slip into the museum and check out that malfunctioning coffeepot outlet.

Chapter Thirteen

Sandi glanced at her watch. Seven-fifteen already? Shadows had grown longer with sunset less than half an hour away, but she'd been so busy she'd totally lost track of time. Where was Cate? She was supposed to have relieved her at six.

The historical society had decided not only to tap into the Fourth of July weekend horse-show crowds with a Navajo taco concession, but into the Main Street throng, as well. Sandi had volunteered to work the Saturday afternoon three-to-six shift at a snow cone concession outside Dix's Woodland Warehouse.

Sharlene, naturally, hadn't bothered to volunteer for anything.

Sandi finished with a customer, then pulled out her cell phone. "Cate? Hi, this is Sandi. At the snow cone stand."

Through the phone a loudspeaker blared in the background.

"Hey, Sandi." Cate sounded a bit breathless. "How are things going? Business is hopping here."

"You're at the horse show?"

"Yeah, these Navajo tacos are one popular item."

Sandi pulled the folded activities schedule from the pocket of her sundress and spread it on the concession stand's counter. "The agenda calls for you to take over here at six. It's past seven. Will you be here soon?"

Dead silence.

"Cate?"

"I'm sorry, Sandi. I must have read it wrong. We have several hours of events yet to go. Twila called in sick, so we're shorthanded."

"You can't come at all?" She glanced at her daughter, wandering over to chat with Sharon Dixon, who manned the sale tables next to them. "I have Gina here with me and it's been a long day for her. I need to get her home and to bed at a decent hour."

"I can't leave here right this minute. Becky had to run to the store for more supplies. Look, let me call around. See if I can find someone to fill in for me here—or there, okay?"

With a not-so-good feeling gnawing in the pit of her stomach, Sandi hung up just as Gina's weary countenance brightened.

"Uncle Bryce! Do you want a snow cone?"

The big bearded man walking along the street's edge turned in their direction. He hesitated, then wove his way through the crowd. Stepped up on the Warehouse's porch and approached.

"Well, look at you, little lady." He tipped his hat back on his head, then his smile broadened as he tugged at a braided pigtail—the kind of smile that made a handsome man even handsomer. "An official snow cone maker."

"Me and Mom have been doing this *all* afternoon." She gave her brow a melodramatic swipe with the back of her cherry syrup-stained hand, then reached for his big one. Sandi cringed inwardly, wishing Gina hadn't taken such an obvious liking to her father's friend. "We sold a billion of them, Uncle Bryce."

"Is that a fact?" He smiled at Sandi, taking in her belted sundress with an approving glance. "Must be the pretty sales staff."

Her heart dipped, capsized, and it was all she could do to meet his gaze. "It's cooling off now, so I don't know how popular something icy will continue to be. But it looks like the pizza vendor up the way is doing a booming business."

"Have you two had dinner?"

That sounded suspiciously like the prelude to an invitation. "Gina has. I'm waiting for our replacement to get here."

His forehead creased. "When's that?"

"Over an hour ago, but she's been delayed."

"I'd be happy to pick up something for you. Just name it."

"Thanks, but someone will be here soon, then we'll head home."

He studied her a moment, almost as if cognizant of being shown the door. He gave Gina's hand a squeeze, then released it. "I need to take care of some business just up the street, but I'll stop back and check on you two in a bit."

He tipped his hat, his dark eyes locking on hers, and turned away to once again step off the porch and into the crowd.

She watched as he wove his way among the milling bodies where the thoroughfare had been closed off to accommodate an evening of old-fashioned square dancing. The sound of a fiddle tuning up tickled her ears.

He'd check on them later.

How long had it been since a man concerned himself about her? Seemed to need reassurance that everything was okay in her world? Ironic, wasn't it, that it appeared to be a man who'd done his best to turn her and Keith's universe upside down?

"You should have let him get you something to eat, doll. Even gone with him." Sharon, straightening outdoor gear on her tables, nodded toward Bryce's retreating form. "I could have watched over things here. He looks like a man who could use some company tonight."

Did he?

"Mommy?" Gina tugged on her skirt. "When's Uncle Bryce going to have kids to keep him company? Maybe I can go fishing with them."

Sandi glanced at Sharon with a little-pitchers-have-big-ears look and slipped an arm around her daughter's shoulders. Sharon had no doubt heard the Uncle

Bryce references, but Sandi'd tired of explaining and had given up correcting Gina.

"Not any time soon, honey. And if and when he ever does have kids, they'll be tiny babies and won't be big enough to go fishing with you right away."

"Oh."

Sandi peeked again at her watch, wishing Arizona went on daylight saving time like most of the country. Even before the sun actually set, the towering ponderosa pines blocked the light still filtering between the western clouds. She didn't look forward to walking along the shadowy, tree-lined mile-and-a-half stretch home.

Early in the afternoon it seemed like a fun adventure to traverse the sun-bathed, graveled road. To avoid the glut of summer visitors fighting for a parking space. She never imagined it would be *dark* by the time they set off…

Nevertheless, the day's effort had been worthwhile and with each coin dropped into the money bag, her spirits had risen. If museum revenues for the day and the horse show concession did as well as the snow cones, they should be good to go on the rent increase next month.

But what about the next one?

And the one after that?

Surely it wouldn't come down to losing the museum while she was president? That she'd have to endure the shame of being at the society's helm should such a disaster happen. She had to trust God on this one, or she'd be up all night worrying about it. Again.

She glanced at her watch once more. Now all she wanted was to get home to the cozy confines of Bradshaws-in-the-Pines.

Before dark.

True to his word, Bryce swung back by the Warehouse thirty minutes later. He waited off to the side, out of the way, as Sandi showed two ladies he recognized from the church how to operate the snow cone machine. Good. Her reinforcements had finally arrived.

Even under the harsh, bare-bulb light of the Warehouse's porch, she sure looked sweet tonight, with shiny hair grazing her cheek and her bare arms toned. Pretty dress, too. Patterned with tiny blue-and-white checks and belted at a trim waist, it draped over her hips and flared into a full skirt that swayed with her every move. He took a deep breath and looked away. He shouldn't be noticing that kind of stuff. Although when he had gotten together with Joe this week, he'd been assured God had designed him to notice, just not to dwell on it or take inappropriate action. He sure was glad Joe understood all this God stuff and was willing to share.

"Earl will be by at ten," Sandi assured the two women. "He'll pick up the money bag and secure everything to use again on Monday."

Taking Gina's hand, she said goodbye to Sharon and

stepped off the porch. He pushed himself away from the stone wall as she approached.

"Oh." She halted. "Bryce."

Was she dismayed to see him? Pleased? He couldn't tell.

"Finishing up for the night? Ready for something to eat?"

"Gina's fading fast. I need to get her tucked in for the night. I'll grab something to eat later."

He glanced down at the sleepy-eyed girl who smiled up at him but without as much wattage as usual.

"I can walk you to your car."

"Thanks, but we didn't drive."

He frowned. "You walked all the way from out on Timber Ridge Road?"

She laughed and his ears welcomed the sound.

"It seemed like a good idea at the time. Having second thoughts now that the sun's set."

"I can give you a ride."

Anxious eyes met his. What was he, a big bad wolf? What kind of stories had Keith and her mother-in-law filled her head with?

She looked down at the weary Gina, then back at him—options considered, the decision made. "If it wouldn't be too much trouble, we'd appreciate it."

"No trouble at all." He picked up the little girl, who weighed about as much as a snowflake. Curled right into his arms as if she belonged there. Poor thing, no way would she make it all the way out to the Bradshaw place on her own two legs, and she was getting too big for Sandi to carry that far. "My SUV's at Grandma's."

Sandi nodded and they headed off along the busy street, skirting vendors and an increasingly boisterous crowd as square-dancing couples in their brightly colored regalia launched into another toe-tapping dance. Neon lights. Popcorn crunching underfoot. The tantalizing scent of pizza, hot dogs and cotton candy. He didn't give much thought to his surroundings, though, being a little too conscious of Sandi at his side and thankful for the opportunity to come to her rescue when it was evident she wasn't keen on walking home alone. For whatever reason, he liked the feeling of being her protector. Her guardian.

Just off Main Street, the short distance down the dimly lit route to Grandma's was a much quieter one. But he hadn't expected to find the side street lined on both sides with bumper-to-bumper cars—and one parked smack across the driveway of the fenced-in yard of the museum. Trapping his SUV.

He surveyed the situation with dismay. No telling when the vehicle's owner would show up again. "Looks like we've encountered one of the hazards of living so close to Main Street when there's a special event."

"I appreciate your offer anyway. I'll call Meg or Sharon."

He needed to tell her about his plans for the museum. Give her a heads-up. Get Grandma off his back. Get it out in the open and over with. No time like the present.

"You have anything against walking? Nice night." He didn't wait for Sandi's response, but patted the leg of the child nestling in his arms. "You ready for a walk home, little gal?"

Gina nodded, settling more deeply into his arms, tucking her head under his neck. His heart reveling in her unhesitant trust made him all the more determined to see them safely to their destination.

"Then let's do it."

Not waiting for her mother's approval, he turned back toward Main Street and started off. But a dozen steps along, not sensing Sandi at his side as she had been before, he halted. Looked back to where she still stood.

Even in the dim light, he could read her almost disoriented expression. Someone else calling the shots tonight left her flummoxed. But he knew better than to laugh.

"You comin'?"

It was warmer than usual this evening, so why was she trembling inside? Even had goose bumps on her arms as if she'd just consumed a gallon of ice cream.

She sensed Bryce looking down at her as they walked beside the starlit road, but she kept her eyes focused on the flashlight-illuminated dimness in front of her, trying to keep her footing on the rutted path. He'd laughed at the miniature, key chain-clipped device she'd pulled from her purse but, hey, it was doing the trick.

"I think Gina's asleep already." His words came softly. "She's breathing pretty steady."

He shifted her daughter in his arms, then let his free hand drop to his side. It brushed hers for a fleeting second, and her heart leaped to an accelerated tempo.

"I should have left her with a sitter, but she wanted to make snow cones. And we never have nearly enough time together to suit me."

"Because of work? I imagine things have been tough financially since you lost Keith."

"God's been faithful. Our needs are more than met. But the part-time Warehouse job picks up some of the extras."

Extras like display cases for the future veterans exhibit at the museum, complete with recessed lighting, adjustable glass shelves, commercial safety glass and keyed security locks. She had them all picked out.

Dare she tell him?

Or would he think her foolish for wanting a memorial to her husband? He didn't seem to think much of what he called "digging through musty old stuff that belonged to dead people." Already told her she needed to get a life.

His hand brushed hers again, all but setting her fingertips on fire, and she eased a bit farther from him. Like a gentleman, he'd taken the traffic side of the road as they'd set off on the uneven shoulder surface. But she'd no more than put some distance between them when she stumbled. His hand shot out, found hers. And without thinking, she grasped it, allowing him to steady her, prevent her from sliding down into the weed-and-rock-filled ditch next to them.

To her alarm, he didn't turn her hand loose once she'd righted herself. She should pull free. Not let her fingers continue to meld into his. But it felt good. Secure and warm. Safe. As though someone cared.

She forced herself to take deep, slow breaths.

"Thanks for walking us home, Bryce."

"Happy to do it." She sensed the smile in his voice. "Need the exercise."

As if he looked as though he needed any more of *that*.

She drank in another lungful of the pine-scented air. "When I first came to Canyon Springs, I couldn't get used to how dark nights get around here."

"That's right. You're a city girl." He jiggled her hand playfully.

The already irregular cadence of her breathing stalled. "Don't laugh, but I'd lie awake at night in the trailer, listening to all the things that go bump in the night. Would convince myself the prisoner who'd escaped two hundred miles from here was standing outside my bedroom window. The stillness freaked me out. And the dark. I didn't think I'd be able to stay here. Especially way out at the trailer."

He didn't respond, except to adjust his clasp on her hand. He probably thought she was a dork. Her confession probably confirmed in his mind that Keith had to put up with more than any man should ever have had to.

"You were afraid," he repeated at long last.

Sensing him gazing down at her, she forced a nervous laugh. "I know it sounds silly, but I can admit it now. I was terrified after Keith and I got married and he left me here alone."

"Did he know that?" An unexpected harshness grazed his tone.

"I knew it would seem silly, so I came up with just about every reason under the sun why he needed to get me out of here—except that one."

"It's not silly to be scared of something that might be worth being scared about. You should have told him."

"He'd have laughed."

"I don't think he'd have laughed."

"No? But you probably would have if he'd have told you. Be honest, you'd have thought I was a big baby making a big deal about nothing."

He seemed to be mulling that one over in his mind. Of course he'd have laughed. Would have used it as ammunition against her. To drive a wedge between her and Keith.

"You still get scared at night?"

His question surprised her. "Sometimes."

Silence hung between them except for the gravel crunching under their feet.

"I can get some motion lights set up at your place if you want me to. You know, the kind that come on if someone walks by? Just put it on your checklist and it's as good as done."

"So every time a skunk strolls past, a spotlight catches him in the act? Thanks, but I'm starting to appreciate the starry skies and the quiet nights."

Up the road headlights punctured the darkness, and in unspoken unison they dropped each other's hand as a rumbling diesel pickup barreled past, illuminating them in a blinding flash.

She took a relieved breath. Good. That was better.

But she hadn't taken half a dozen steps, her eyes still adjusting once more to the darkness, when his big hand caught hers again.

Chapter Fourteen

"I don't want you to be afraid, Sandi."

He gave the soft fingers tucked in his a gentle squeeze. He wouldn't allow it. Not if there was anything he could do about it.

Sandi had been scared.

That's why she'd nagged Keith about moving. About relocating to a bigger community. Closer to her family in Missouri. Not because she was a spoiled, bossy brat, but because she was scared. When Keith had mentioned his concerns about his bride's objections to Canyon Springs, Bryce told his buddy in no uncertain terms he shouldn't let her push him around, that she'd married him for better or for worse. Needed to learn who wore the pants in the family. She should stop her whining and stay put right where he'd left her.

But she'd been scared.

What a world-class jerk I've been, Lord.

She'd been pregnant that first year, too. In a town filled with strangers. Far from family. The situation probably hadn't improved much even when Gina came along, but she hadn't wanted to admit her fear. Didn't want Keith—*and his best buddy*—to think her silly.

"Thank you again, Bryce, for seeing us home."

Her soft voice interrupted his self-condemnation as she slipped her hand from his, leaving his own feeling empty. Bereft. But they'd already come to the driveway of her fenced-in yard, and she was right. It was pitch-dark out here.

"I can drive you back to town," she offered.

"Thanks, but you need to get Gina to bed. I wasn't making it up when I said I need the exercise. I'm trying to keep in shape for firefighter quals. I'm wearing tennies tonight, so I'll jog back."

"Are you sure?"

"I'm sure."

They stood for an awkward moment, as if both waiting for the other to say something more. Then she led the way up the short drive to the bottom of the front deck's steps.

"I can take my sleepyhead daughter now."

Loath to turn loose of the sweet, warm weight cradled in his arms, he nodded toward the door. "Let me get her up the stairs for you."

Sandi moved ahead of him to unlock the entrance, then turned toward him once again.

"I enjoyed our walk, Sandi."

"Me, too."

Could she hear his heart pounding? Sense his nervousness? This had all the makings of first-date ill-at-ease goodbyes. He couldn't see the details of her face, her expression, in the tree-shadowed dimness, but only an idiot wouldn't have been aware of the voltage crackling between them.

He leaned down…and slipped Gina into her arms. Straightened up and stepped away.

"So, Sandi," he said, attempting to bring his pulse rate back into the normal range. He *would* have to go and notice how good she smelled when he bent to deposit Gina into her embrace. "What are you still doing here? In Canyon Springs?"

He heard a quick intake of breath. Then after a long moment her words came softly. "I'm here because it's what Keith wanted."

"But it wasn't what you wanted."

"No. Not at the beginning. But this is where he wanted to raise Gina. And it's where I hope, in some small way, to honor him in a community he loved."

"I don't understand."

"I haven't told anyone else." She paused again, as if debating what she intended to share next. "But I'm determined to convince the historical society to turn that back bedroom, the one we use for storage, into an exhibit to honor local military veterans. And to get them to name it in memory of Keith. I've been saving for quality display cases for years, hoping that will nudge them in the right direction."

An invisible hand socked him in the gut.

Great. Just great.

But right now didn't seem like the time to tell her that wasn't going to happen.

"That's very noble, Sandi."

"Noble? No. It's the least I can do for Keith. For his mom." Gina stirred in her arms. "I guess I'd better get her inside. Good night, Bryce. And thank you again for seeing us home."

"My pleasure." He tipped his hat as he held the door open for her. Saw her safely inside.

When she closed it and he heard the dead bolt slide home, he whipped off his hat, trotted down the wooden steps—and took off running.

Had the jog back to town enabled Bryce to sleep any better than she had?

Disgruntled, her insides still quaking like an aspen leaf, Sandi pulled a wicker picnic basket—a much-used wedding present—from a shelf in the hall closet and carried it to the kitchen table. At church that morning the Diaz family had invited her and Gina to join them for a cookout early this evening—to which she'd agreed only after making sure a certain some-one hadn't been invited, as well.

Tomorrow was the fifth anniversary of Keith's death. Fourth of July. No doubt the tenderhearted Meg remembered and wanted to make certain she had something to do to keep her mind occupied. Along the same lines, LeAnne's kids had insisted their mother spend the holiday weekend with them in the Valley.

She shook her head. Were they a pitiful pair or what?

A guilty pang stung her conscience. She hadn't been thinking of Keith today, but Bryce. Not remembering how Keith had kissed her, but wondering what it might be like to kiss a certain big, bearded army sergeant.

To her annoyance, she'd tossed and turned for hours last night. Relived over and over what she'd said, what he'd said, attempted to reconstruct the walk home from start to finish. What was she anyway? Sixteen?

She pulled from the refrigerator a sealed container of the now-chilled macaroni salad she'd made earlier that afternoon. Wrapped it securely in a tea towel so it wouldn't sweat, and slipped it into the oversize basket. A jar of dill spears followed. A container of freshly baked chocolate chip cookies. Woven paper plate holders. A bag of potato chips.

Should she stop by Wyatt's Grocery for a jug of juice for the kids?

Her mind unwillingly tracked once again to last evening. Had Bryce taken her hand prior to or after she told him about being afraid in Canyon Springs? If it was after, his reaching out to her meant he only felt sorry for her. No, wait. Didn't he take her hand before that? Even before the speeding truck came along? She'd been so shocked at his boldness, so confused, so tingling all over that her brain had gone into meltdown mode, muddling the minutes between town and the trailer.

But one thing that wasn't muddled was the memory of him as they reached the trailer door. Him holding

Gina. Standing too close. Bending down toward her. How certain she'd been that he intended to kiss her—and she'd had no intention of resisting.

Had she totally lost her mind?

Of course the man had no intention of kissing her. She had to get hold of herself. Stop indulging in daydreams. She didn't need a man in her life right now. And certainly not Bryce Harding. In fact, in the years since Keith's death, not once had she become romantically involved.

Hadn't dated. Not one single time.

Always begged off, had other plans. Friends cajoled and plotted to set her up with their male friends, but she managed to—gracefully for the most part—decline. But she couldn't tell anyone the truth—that she didn't deserve another chance at a happily ever after. Or why. She was too ashamed to confess her despicably immature behavior to anyone but God. Confess how Keith had carried to the grave her parting words as his last memory of her.

She had no business ruining another man's life, potentially hurting him as she had Keith. Not even the life of a man like Bryce who'd done his best to ruin hers.

But oh, those twinkling brown eyes…

"Hey, you! Big ugly dude!"

Bryce jerked his head up from where he bent over his fishing boat, securing it to the trailer after an afternoon of fishing at Casey Lake.

Bumping back his Western hat with a wrist, he scanned the immediate area and beyond, trying to pinpoint the voice. Quite a few people out on a holiday weekend. None seemed to be paying attention to him.

"Yeah, you!" the voice came again. "Get yourself over here and join us for burgers."

Then Bryce spotted Joe Diaz manning a grill back in the shadows of a stand of ponderosa pines. Meg was busy arranging picnic items on the open tailgate of their pickup. He grinned and returned a wave.

He didn't want to horn in on a family outing but, as hungry as he was and with Grandma Mae dining with one of her friends tonight, Joe wouldn't have to ask him twice.

He finished securing the boat, then got in his SUV and pulled both into a space reserved for boat trailers. He'd no more than set foot out of the pickup when seemingly out of nowhere a pigtailed little girl launched herself at him. "Uncle Bryce!"

Instinctively, his eyes sought out her mother.

And there she was. Strolling from the far side of the parking lot with a wicker picnic basket over her arm, a breeze ruffling her hair.

His heartbeat quickened as he picked up Gina and headed toward the picnic area. Would Sandi approach him first? Wait for him to approach her? What would she be thinking, expecting, after he'd grabbed hold of her hand last night? Did she even realize how close she'd come to getting kissed?

How he hated leaving her alone at that trailer last night. But the way the sparks were flying between them, New Bryce knew he didn't dare set foot through the door to carry Gina to her room.

He'd run all the way back to Gran's. Hard. If anyone had seen him, they'd have suspected bloodhounds on his heels. But even after that exertion, he'd hardly slept, the reality of his misconceptions about Sandi's motivations slamming home again and again.

She'd been scared.

God, please forgive me for being so callous. And for the way I'm starting to feel about Keith's wife.

He had no business feeling *anything* for his buddy's bride beyond brotherly concern. But by the time they'd reached her place last night, her hand tucked in his, he'd wanted to take her in his arms. Hold her close. Protect her.

Gina toyed with his T-shirt collar, bringing him back to the present, her eyes gazing confidently into his. "Mommy says you carried me all the way home."

"I did at that."

She shook her head. "I don't remember. I was sleeping."

"Yeah, you were."

When they reached the picnic table she gave him a hug, then wiggled until he set her back on the ground. Meg and Joe smiled at him. Actually, Joe smirked. Had he heard the Uncle Bryce thing? But Sandi, pretty in a pink top and figure-skimming jeans, focused on unpacking the picnic basket at the far end of the table.

"Hey, Sandi."

She looked up. Smiled. Mouthed a "hi" and returned to her work.

He stood awkwardly for a moment, then sat down at the opposite end of the table with Davy, who animatedly related all the things he'd done that day. Gina joined them and put in her two cents' worth. But although he listened and responded, with his fine-tuned internal radar and the corner of his eye, he kept track of Sandi's every move.

Playing it cool, was she?

But it was no wonder she thought it better to pretend he didn't exist. He shouldn't have taken her hand last night. A simple "be careful there" when she stumbled would have sufficed. But no, he liked the feeling of her soft fingers clasped in his. Made him feel strong and protective. So he'd kept her hand there, even when she'd been in no danger.

But like it or not, at the first opportunity he'd tell her about his plans for the museum. Wouldn't put it off any longer. He'd probably get kicked in the shin, but at least he'd get it over with and Grandma would stop her nagging.

Relieved when Joe's "come and get it" drew everyone to the tailgate sideboard, he held back, waiting for the kids and gals to serve themselves first. Then when they'd been seated under the trees, he moseyed on over to fill his own plate.

"Sooo, what's up with you and Sandi?" Joe joined him at the pickup's tailgate, his voice low.

"What do you mean? Because Gina calls me Uncle Bryce? No big deal. I told her I was like a brother to her dad. That means an uncle in six-year-old logic."

"No, there's more to it than that. I mean you're looking at Sandi when she's not looking and she's looking at you when you're not looking. Gotta be something going on."

Was she checking him out when he wasn't looking? "Eyes gotta go someplace, don't they?"

"Right." Joe unfolded the aluminum foil-wrapped burgers and speared several with a fork. "She's a nice gal. Pretty lady."

"Suppose so."

Joe snorted, then arranged tomato and lettuce on low-fat-mayo-slathered buns. "Listen to you. Like you think I believe you haven't noticed she's a looker? Not buyin' that one. Stop hanging out here like a hog at a trough and get yourself on over there. Strike up a conversation."

Hog at a trough? Joe should talk. He'd already loaded up three burgers to Bryce's two.

"Come on, Joe. Knock it off. She was my best friend's wife. Tomorrow it will be five years since he was killed in action."

"So? She's nobody's wife now, is she?" Joe turned

to ensure his back was to the others, his voice still low. "Look, I'm going to tell you the same thing Dad told me last year when I was dragging my feet about Meg."

"You dragged your feet with a woman like Meg?" He glanced over at the sassy brunette chatting with Sandi, then shot Joe a disbelieving look. "You're that dense, and you have the gall to think you can coach me about *my* love life?"

Joe grimaced. "Look, it's a long story. But it came down to my dad flat out telling me I was as dumb as a rock if I didn't move in before some other guy did. And I'm telling you the same thing. God gave you a brain, use it."

"Nice theory, but there's a slight problem."

"I know. I'm looking at him."

"Funny." He took a deep breath and helped himself to the macaroni salad. "It's just this—I didn't want Keith to marry her."

"Ohhh," Joe groaned softly. "Now I get it. A love triangle. You both liked her and she picked him."

"No, I mean I didn't like her. At all. And I tried to talk him out of marrying her for that same reason."

"Does she know that?"

"That's part of the problem."

Joe gave a low whistle. "Now that *is* a problem."

"Told you."

Joe pulled a handful of chips from an open bag and

deposited them on his plate, his brow crinkling. "So why didn't you like her? Explain that to me."

He was beginning to wonder the same thing himself, so how could he explain it?

"Don't have all night, *hog*." Bryce elbowed his way past Joe and headed toward the picnic table.

Chapter Fifteen

"Here he comes, here he comes," Meg said, her voice low and lips barely moving. "I'm outta here."

"Wait, don't—"

But her friend snatched up her plate and joined the kids who were digging through one of the coolers at the other end of the table as if mining for gold. "Hey, hey," she teased, "what are you two looking for?"

Had Meg planned this? Or was Bryce's fishing outing at Casey Lake mere coincidence?

She glanced up as he rounded the table, loaded plate in hand. How handsome he looked, the black No Regrets T-shirt emphasizing the span of his shoulders, the rock-solid biceps.

"Mind if I join you?" With a tip of his hat, dark eyes focused on her uncertainly.

"Not at all. Have a seat." She lifted the lid to her hamburger bun and self-consciously rearranged the lettuce. The tomato. Felt the table shift as he seated himself. Got comfortable. "I didn't see you at church this morning."

He studied her as if trying to figure out whether not seeing him was a good thing—or bad.

"Took Grandma out to Bill Diaz's RV park for the Fourth of July service." He spread the paper napkin on his lap. "Then we stuck around to help him and Sharon Dixon serve breakfast."

"I didn't know Joe's dad held church services out there."

"Not every weekend. But Bill's ex-navy, as was his son and father, so he invites his campground residents to take part in outdoor worship the Sunday closest to Independence Day."

"Your grandpa was in the military, too, wasn't he?" She speared an evasive macaroni noodle, relieved he'd allowed the conversation to focus on the mundane, not on the supercharged evening before. "I seem to remember Mae telling me that."

"Yeah, U.S. Army like me. The military seems to run in families around here." He glanced to where Joe and Meg were picking up their filled plates and moving away from the table. Where were they going? "After the worship service Bill treats his guests to a home-cooked breakfast—pancakes and sausage, fresh fruit. Nothing fancy, but Grandma's helped out for years."

"Sounds nice. I'm surprised Meg and Joe didn't go. I talked to them at church this morning."

"They went, just didn't hang around for breakfast."

She nodded.

They ate in fairly solid silence, between bites both gazing around self-consciously at the lakeside setting. Occasional two-or three-word comments. Good burgers. Nice weather. Monsoons coming soon.

Joe had spread a tarp under one of the trees some distance from them to ensure the long, pokey pine needles littering the ground wouldn't cause discomfort, then threw an old blanket over the top of it. Now he and Meg were cozied up as she teasingly fed him one potato chip at a time. The kids, spread out on the blanket, giggled as he wiggled his eyebrows at them.

"So, Sandi." Bryce, having downed his second burger, pushed back his plate and broke the silence. "There's something we need to talk about."

She paused, the last bite of her hamburger halfway to her mouth. She'd heard the phrase "felt the blood drain from her face," and now she knew the reality of it. Was he going to apologize for last night? Tell her— what? That there was no way he'd get involved with a woman like her and he didn't want that hand-holding business to create any misunderstandings?

She placed the hamburger on her plate. Said a prayer. Forced a smile as she met his solemn-eyed gaze. "And what might that be?"

"Uncle Bryce! Uncle Bryce!"

A giggling Davy and Gina pounced on him from behind, looping their arms around him as far as they could reach.

His gaze flashed briefly to hers, apologetic. Then he

laughed, eyes now twinkling as he turned to embrace both of them, one in each arm. "What's all this?"

"Take us out in your boat. Please?" Gina's words came breathlessly. "We want to fish."

"Now, Gina—" She frowned her disapproval at the interruption. What had Bryce intended to say?

Bryce gave her daughter's shoulder a gentle pat. "I'd be happy to take you out, but your mom has to come along, too." He craned his neck to look pointedly at Sandi. "Like I told you before, no kids without another grown-up."

No way was *she* going. "Maybe Joe will go."

Gina had set her heart on fishing, but when she discovered it wasn't what she imagined, she'd stop harping about it. Kids didn't understand it involved sitting still, being quiet and waiting for something that may or may not happen. Patience wasn't Gina's most notable characteristic.

Bryce nodded to where Meg's husband had sacked out on the blanket, his head in his wife's lap. "Joe? Not likely."

Gina pulled away from Bryce and ran to her mother's side. Eyes dancing. Hopeful. Looking so much like her daddy. "Please, Mommy? Davy's mom said he could go."

Then shouldn't Meg be the one to climb into a rocking boat and set out for deep water? Her stomach did an uneasy somersault. She didn't want to go out in a boat.

"I have life jackets for everybody now." Bryce

raised a brow, eyes twinkling and his tone challenging. "Even kid-size ones."

"I suppose—"

"Thank you, Mommy." Gina threw her arms around her for a hug. "Come on Davy, let's go!"

"Wait, wait." Sandi caught Gina's arm before she took off for the water. "Settle down. I'm sure Uncle Bryce has some rules we need to follow."

She turned to him expectantly—and caught his unabashed grin. He'd heard her call him Uncle Bryce. Shaking her head in defeat, she shot him a wait-until-I-get-my-hands-on-your-throat look.

Thirty minutes later he had the fishing boat in the water, life jackets secured and the electric motor silently propelling them across the wet, glassy surface.

In the bow she gripped the bench seat, anxiously keeping an eye on Gina and Davy as the boat skimmed across the lake. Bryce gave her a reassuring nod, but why couldn't they stick closer to shore? Why'd they have to go so far out?

He'd already warned them that sound magnifies, carries across on the water, so they needed to keep their voices down. They didn't want to disturb the other fishermen.

The children had nodded solemnly, Davy chiming in with "Grandpa says you can scare the fishes away, too."

This late in the day, even with sunset ninety minutes away, the sun had dipped behind the pine tree tops, stretching shade across the lake. Bryce cut the motor, and the water around them calmed as the boat gently rocked. No speedboats were allowed on the lake, no gas-powered motors to disturb the stillness.

He nodded to Gina as he pulled out a fishing rod from the floor of the boat and rummaged in an old metal tackle box. "Your dad and I used to come out to this lake and fish all day."

"You did?" she whispered. "You and Daddy had a boat?"

"Borrowed one."

"How old were you? My age?"

"A bit older." He winked at Sandi as he patiently explained to the kids the purpose of the bobber, then baited a hook with a ripe-smelling, lime-green goop that he assured would make a trout's mouth water.

Sandi wrinkled her nose. To each his own.

With expertise born of years of fishing, off to the side of the boat Bryce whipped the rod and set the clear line sailing above the water with a soft whirring sound. When the weight hit the surface with a pleasant, hollow *thunk,* generating ever-expanding circular ripples, he handed the rod to Davy. The boy took it with the seriousness of a pro.

He reached for another rod. "You ready to try, Gina?"

Her daughter's jerky nod proved her excitement.

Sandi closed her eyes and lifted her face to the sky, listening as Bryce answered Gina's never-ending battery of questions. Letting the coolish breeze touch her cheek. Drinking in the slightly fishy lake-water scent. Although others fished along the shore and on boats scattered across the lake, it was as if she, Bryce and the kids were cocooned in a blanket of peace. So still out here. So tranquil. Her fingers relaxed—somewhat—on the bench seat.

How many times had she watched Keith practice casting with his rod and reel? Too many times to count. That man lived to fish. Was his gear still in the shed in back of the trailer? Maybe Bryce would like to have it.

As much as she hated to admit it, she was beginning to understand why he and Keith had become fast friends. Both outdoorsmen. Subtle sense of humor. Good with kids. Possessing an underlying sensitivity that belied their rough-and-tough exteriors. Knowing both the good and the bad in the other, they remained unconditionally loyal. Lifetime friends.

Had she ever had a friend—*been* a friend—quite like that?

She opened her eyes when she heard the whir of the reel, watched as Bryce carefully showed Gina how to hold the rod. Again explained the process. He caught Sandi's eye. Smiled.

Her heart unaccountably skittering, she smiled back.

"I never understood the appeal of catching some smelly little critter with fins. But this is so relaxing. Your mind can just drift. And look at that sky."

He looked upward, as well, studying the towering cumulus clouds with their billowing dimensions. Pristine white. Slate blue. An array of deep violet, mauve, lavender. Hot pink. All trimmed in a glowing gold where the sun pierced through.

"God paints portraits of his love on the sky, that's for sure."

Surprised, she turned to look at him. "That's a beautiful way of putting it."

"Hey, even a crusty old fisherman can harbor the soul of a poet under a sky like that."

Their gazes held as if secured by an invisible magnet. The seconds ticking, communicating silently a mutual curiosity, uncertainty. Unconcealed interest.

Every fiber of her nervous system all but sizzling, she refocused her attention on her daughter, a desperate attempt to smother what she refused to acknowledge. "You're a born fisherman, just like your daddy."

Gina turned to her, eyes bright. "I am?"

She nodded. Who'd have thought Gina could sit so still for this long? Whisper and not shout? And who'd have thought she'd ever find herself looking at Bryce Harding like *that*? She tightened her grip on the bench seat, not allowing her gaze to drift to the big, bearded man at the far end of the boat.

"Your daddy always wanted me to go fishing with him."

"Did you?"

"No. I'm not a good swimmer. Makes me nervous when I know I can't touch the bottom and still keep my head above water."

"You should have said something." Concern clouded

Bryce's dark eyes. "Do you want me to move closer to shore?"

She shook her head. Gave him a carefully controlled smile. "No, that's okay. The water's still. And I have the life jacket. If I go overboard, though, you'll have to fish me out."

He nodded, his eyes still troubled. "You can count on it."

"Mommy says I swim better than a fish," Gina piped up in her big outside voice—and Davy shushed her. She cringed. Nodded. Went silent.

"That so?" Bryce took off his hat, wiped his forehead with his hand, then settled the hat back on his head.

"I made sure she started lessons when she was a toddler. I didn't want her to be wary of water like her mother."

"Shhhh," Gina reminded, putting a finger to her lips. "You're scaring my fish."

Sandi made an "excuse *me*" face at Bryce. He grinned and an absurd sense of contentment filled her.

"Do you want to fish, too?" he whispered from the far side of the boat. "I've got an extra rod tucked back in here. Might make a fisherwoman of you yet."

"Don't count on it." But it did have an appeal—as long as she didn't catch anything.

To her relief, though, he didn't push. Didn't insist she give it a try. Didn't make fun of her. Didn't get disgruntled the way most men would have at her refusal.

Even Keith had gotten put out a time or two about it, which wasn't his nature.

He'd put up with a lot.

Maybe, in some small way, the museum dedication would make it up to him.

It wasn't his imagination. Bryce was sure of it.

He'd seen it in her eyes at the lake a few days ago. Didn't think she could have missed it in his, either. But she'd shut it down fast. Refusing to recognize it. Refusing to admit it. Determined not to let it lead to anything more.

Which was probably the direction he should take, too. That is, if he still had a lick of sense left in him after her big beautiful eyes clearly spelled out her interest in him.

What was a man supposed to do when a woman looked at him like that? Well, he knew what Old Bryce would do, but that was beside the point.

He rubbed his hand along the back of his neck and let out a gust of pent-up breath, his mind's eye—every fiber of his body—reliving that unanticipated connection with the pretty gal sitting in the bow of his boat. Bundled up in her bright orange life jacket. Hands gripping the seat. Her gaze locked on his as they'd all but stared into each other's soul.

Shaking his head, he focused again on the spreadsheets illuminated on the computer screen in front of him. Not looking good. But the fire chief was pushing the city hard to release funds for the empty firefighter opening. He'd used two simultaneous fires last week to press his point. They needed that extra man.

He pushed back in his chair. For weeks he'd been intending to talk to Sandi about his plans for the museum. How he needed to get Grandma Mae down to the lower level. It would break Sandi's heart, what with her determination to set up some kind of memorial for Keith. But what other choice did he have? Grandma could sell the house and get a single-level one, but with the market as it was right now she wouldn't get anywhere near what it would have garnered just a few years ago, before the economy staggered. A newer place would cost more, too, so that meant debt.

Besides, who would buy this place and retain the museum anyway? The historical society sure couldn't swing it.

So his best bet was to give the society ample warning. Then get to work on a downstairs living quarters. Remodel it for handicapped accessibility as time and money allowed—and hope it would be ready before Grandma had a real need for it. Although with those steep stairs she'd already become a prisoner in her own home when no one was around to assist her. Had already lost her independence. No easy thing to accept for a spunky, on-the-go woman who'd never let her age slow her down until now.

Grandma was his first priority. He loved her. Would

care for her to the best of his ability. As much has he hated to disrupt Sandi's plans to honor Keith, that was the way it had to be.

He'd find her and tell her.

Today.

Chapter Sixteen

Things didn't look good.

Sandi stared at the laptop screen, again, studying the spreadsheet that the historical society treasurer had emailed her. While the Fourth of July push to beef up their bank account was encouragingly successful, it fell far short of seeing them through the winter without city assistance. Which meant another fundraiser on the heels of the last. And another after that. It looked as if that would be a regular endeavor from here on out.

If the historical society went under, how would she live it down? How could she prove to LeAnne that her son hadn't made a mistake marrying her?

Although that was debatable.

Get one thing straight, Keith. If you're determined to make the military a lifelong career, you can forget about having any more children. At least with me, anyway.

All the excuses in the world couldn't make up for

those hateful words—not Gina being sick at the time, not living far away from all that was familiar, not fear for Keith's safety. She could justify her rejecting, wounding words any way she wanted to, but it came down to pure selfishness and not trusting God.

She pushed back from the kitchen table to watch Gina playing on the sofa with her plastic horses. Galloping. Neighing. At least she'd finally put aside the makeshift fishing pole she'd insisted Mommy make from a sturdy long stick and heavy string weighted by a magnet. Construction-paper fish with paper clip "hooks" made for several days of fishing fun, and Gina had talked nonstop about Uncle Bryce and the real-life fish she'd caught.

Bryce.

Her mind's eye flickered to the big man. The engaging grin that split his bearded face. The gentle, expressive eyes. The way he'd looked at her when out on the lake. She couldn't deny it—she'd looked right back at him with every bit as much boldness as he had her. Had allowed her fingers to linger in his palm as he helped her step from the boat back to shore. Had rested her hand on his rock-solid arm when thanking him for taking the kids fishing.

He probably thought Keith's widow was coming on to him.

Was she?

She pondered the unpretentious floral arrangement sitting on the living room coffee table. Red and white carnations with blue ribbons. She'd found it outside the front door when she'd awakened on Independence Day—a note from Bryce tucked in the foliage, expressing his sympathy at her loss.

As much as she'd loved Keith, it wasn't inconceivable that Bryce had lost more than she had. They'd been friends since grade school. She'd known him only four years, the first two courting by email and phone calls, and the latter two without significantly more in-person contact than the first two.

Did Bryce have any idea how right he'd been to try to keep Keith from marrying her those many years ago? Every time she saw him, she couldn't help but wonder…had her husband told him of her appalling ultimatum?

She turned again to her laptop. Like it or not, she had to approach Bryce for an extension on the rent increase. But what were the odds he'd give it to her? He said he'd raised it because he didn't have any choice, was making do with odd jobs while waiting for the firefighter opening. But maybe she could convince him that if the museum closed, the extra money would be cut off until he could find another renter. Something that might not be easy to do with summer half over.

How she hated to face him, beg for a favor after their encounter on Sunday. He'd think she'd had it planned all along, to catch his eye. Butter him up.

But what choice did she have?

She'd find him and ask him.

Today.

* * *

"I'm sorry, Sandi, but I can't go beyond July 31 when the current lease runs out."

On the heels of a lightning flash, a rumbling tremor of thunder rattled spoons on the table. Lights flickered.

From the look on her face where she sat across from him at Kit's Lodge, his words weren't what she hoped to hear. But finalizing calculations for a remodel proved the endeavor could cost considerably more than he'd anticipated. Would take longer, as well, which meant he might need to start on it in the spring, not wait until next summer or the following autumn.

Sandi gripped the newly drawn-up paperwork, her blue eyes flaring but voice even. "What's this with a *one*-month-at-a-time lease? What happened to the year?"

"You know Grandma Mae hurt herself last fall."

Her brow crinkled. "Right. So?"

"So I need to get her out of the apartment and into a place where she can regain some independence. That place is the first floor of her house. The museum."

Sandi's eyes widened. "You're kicking us out?"

"Not right away. Spring maybe. But I'm keeping my options open with a short-term lease. Renewable monthly, of course."

She shook the papers, her voice escalating a notch. "That's why you raised the rent, isn't it? You thought we'd voluntarily pick up and move on our own. Get ourselves out of your hair."

He shook his head. "Since I haven't landed that position I told you about, I need help to cover the re-modeling costs. To make the place handicap accessible. Ramps. Bathroom and kitchen redo. Window replacement. It's a lot more expensive than I thought it would be."

Her eyes flashed every bit as fiercely as the lightning outside the window, catching him off-guard. Had Keith ever been the unlucky recipient of a look like that?

She tossed the papers to the table and crossed her arms. "So it's up to the museum to foot the bill for your dream home, is it?"

He said a silent prayer and kept his tone gentle, determined not to follow her fiery lead. "You've got to admit what the historical society has been paying Grandma the past fifteen years is almost criminal."

Her gaze sparked again as she drew in a sharp breath, opened her mouth—then abruptly closed it. She had to know what rents ran in this tourist town. In a good year, when seasonal visitors overflowed, Grandma could easily have rented the downstairs for the three summer months alone and made far more than what the historical society paid for a full year.

"She never complains." His words came softly, recognizing that although he'd thought it through for months, this was the first time Sandi was hearing anything about his plans. "But Grandma's miserable trapped upstairs. Doesn't like calling on me or a friend every time she wants to enjoy her porch. Go to the grocery store. To church. She can still drive, but negotiating those stairs is too dangerous. She could break her neck. It's only the price tag preventing me from moving ahead on a remodel right now."

"Mae's always been so self-sufficient." The fire in Sandi's eyes dimmed and he breathed a little easier.

"Right. So I've got to get her down to ground level."

Sandi leaned forward, her gaze intent. Challenging. "Then buy a single-story home, Bryce. Keep renting us the museum. Rent out the apartment, too."

Leave it to Little Bossy Boots to think he hadn't already considered those options.

"I don't have that kind of money, Sandi, to own two properties. The best I'd be able to do is sell the museum for far less than it was worth just a few years ago, but then I'd have a higher mortgage payment on a newer place and still have upgrade costs to make it accessible."

She stared at the lease papers fanned across the table, the spark draining out of her. Did the museum really mean that much to her?

"I'm sorry, Sandi. Like I said before, I don't have any choice."

"I know." She didn't look at him, choosing instead to gaze out the window at the restaurant's treed parking lot just as the first of the summer's monsoon rains broke loose from the darkened heavens.

A smattering of applause and cheers echoed around the room as dining locals welcomed the annual downpour. A respite from the heat. Guardian against devastating bark beetles and of the fire-prone forest they lived in and loved.

He didn't join in, but instead studied Sandi. The slump of her shoulders. The quiver of her lower lip. Her resignation killed him. He could handle differences of opinion, objections, even her bossing. But seeing the blaze in her eyes doused to cold ash?

"If you have any other ideas, Sandi," he prodded, "I'm willing to listen."

Come on, let's see a little fight here.

He had no idea she'd take it this hard. Grandma was right. He should have manned up and told her months ago what he was planning. But he hadn't much fancied a confrontation with her. Had put off his announcement too long.

With a quick, decisive motion she turned from the rain-streaming window to gather the lease papers. Slid them into her tote bag. Pulled out her compact umbrella and placed it on the table. "I guess I need to let the society members know. Face the music."

He reached across the table to grasp her hand, which still rested on the umbrella. "This isn't your fault. It isn't even *my* fault."

She shot him a you-can't-be-serious look.

He frowned. "If Sharlene and the others want to blame you, I'll bear the brunt of it. Just send them to me. I'll handle them."

She stared down at his hand on hers.

"I understand why you're mad at me," he continued, his voice low, barely heard above the pounding storm.

Come on, admit it, woman. Show me you're mad. Get that fire blazing in your eyes again. Punch me in the nose or something.

Anything.

"I'm not mad at you."

She bestowed a half smile, but her eyes reflected a sadness, a defeat he couldn't fathom. Weeks ago he'd tactlessly told her she needed to get a life, but he had no idea of the intensity of her attachment to the museum. Was it because she had her heart so set on that memorial to Keith?

"How can I be mad at you knowing you're doing what you think is best for your grandma?" She slipped her hand from his. "And you're right. What the historical society was paying is far below the going rate around here. We were cheating Mae and getting away with it."

"I wouldn't put it in that harsh of terms. There was no intent to do her harm." He drew back his hand. "But look, Sandi, there are other places the museum could move. It's not like you have to close it down."

She stared out the window again, rivulets on the glass obscuring the view. "Even with the increase on the place we have now, it doesn't come near what it could cost to rent a smaller space."

"We'll figure something out."

A disbelieving brow rose as she turned to him. "We?"

He spread his hands in surrender. "Hey, I'm willing to pitch in, help scout out a new location. It's not like you have to find one by next week, right? When summer visitors leave, townsfolk will feel the pinch again, then you can probably negotiate something more palatable to the society's pocketbook."

"You think so?"

An ember sparked in her eyes. Tiny for sure, but he fanned the flame.

"I know so."

A halfhearted laugh didn't reassure him.

"Wish I had your optimism."

"You'll get yours back." She had to. He couldn't stand it if she didn't. "I kind of landed a big one on you this morning. I apologize. I should have said something earlier."

"You tried to at the lake, didn't you? Right before Gina and Davy pounced on you about fishing." She dipped her chin down and tilted her head to look over at him. The familiar mannerism pierced his heart as uncertain, questioning eyes fixed on him.

"Thank you for the flowers."

"You're welcome. The anniversary of Keith's death has to be a hard time for you."

She nodded. "But it gets easier with each passing year."

He nodded. "How's Keith's mom doing?"

"Ups and downs. She went to the Valley for the holiday weekend. That was best." She toyed with the strap of her tote bag, fingers trembling ever so slightly until she fisted her hand to still the giveaway quaver. "My faith's gotten me through it. God's grace. But

LeAnne refuses to acknowledge Anyone exists in the spiritual realm. Which makes it so much harder on her—and on me."

"I can understand that."

With a deep intake of breath, she sat up straighter as if coming to a decision. Zipped her jacket. Gathered the tote bag, purse and umbrella. Stood. "Sorry to run. I have a few things to take care of before I go to work this afternoon."

He stood, too, not ready for her to depart so abruptly. He wanted to tell her about how his faith sustained him, too. About the role her husband had played in that part of his life.

Old Bryce. New Bryce.

"You may as well wait until the storm blows through."

But she only gave him a too-bright smile. Said a quick goodbye and headed toward the restaurant's door.

He remained standing, watching her through the window as, jacket hood up and open umbrella in hand, she dashed across the puddling parking lot to her car. Then, heart heavy, he again lowered himself into his chair and motioned to the waitress for a refill.

"We're losing the museum," Sandi stated flatly to her mother-in-law Friday night after Gina had been put to bed. Under a canopy of stars, monsoon rains long gone until tomorrow, the pair settled into lawn chairs on the front deck. She drank in the sweet scent of rain-washed pine.

LeAnne stirred her iced tea. "What do you mean?"

Her mother-in-law couldn't care less about the museum—although she might if she knew the plans Sandi had for it. But there was no point in telling her about that now. Not with the whole thing set to collapse in spite of Bryce's confident statements that they'd find an alternate location. He was trying to make her feel better. Get himself off the bad-guy hook.

"The Hardings are remodeling the building so Mae, Bryce's grandma, can move downstairs."

"Can they do that? You have a lease, don't you?"

"We do. But it's up for renewal. And if we sign, it's only good for a month at a time until they're ready to start construction."

LeAnne motioned impatiently. "Who in their right mind would sign something like that? What's the point?"

Sandi sighed and stretched out her legs, pointed her toes. "I ran it by the historical society board last night and they agreed it's our only option right now. Sign for a month at a time, knowing we need to have something else lined up by spring."

Setting her tea glass on the glass-topped table between them, LeAnne's tone softened. "I'm sorry about this, honey. I know what great store you put in that place. But this should come as no surprise. I told you, didn't I, that Bryce would be up to no good? He's been muddying the waters since he was a kid."

"I don't think he has any choice, LeAnne. His grandma can't stay in that apartment upstairs much longer. She was hurt badly last year in a fall, and he's concerned she could take another tumble."

"Concerned? If you want my opinion, he's shoving the museum out so he can fix the place up, sell it and pocket the old girl's money."

"I don't think so."

LeAnne again picked up her tea, nails tapping lightly on the glass. Click. Click. Click. "Sweetheart, I hope that you're not developing an attachment to Bryce. He doesn't hold a candle to your husband. And certainly isn't father material for your daughter."

Memory flashed to the night he returned Gina's cap. The way he'd followed through on her checklist. Walked her home. Had looked after her out on the lake. "He's actually—"

"I know you're vulnerable, lonely, but don't fool yourself. Sure, he's big and brawny. A good-looking guy with that hero aura all over him." LeAnne laughed. "I'm sure it proves useful when he's trying to pick up ladies down at the local bar. But do we really know why he so abruptly left the military? Hmm? Highly suspicious."

"It's my understanding he was already leaning toward not reenlisting when his grandma fell. So he came back here to take care of her."

LeAnne sighed. "Honestly, Sandi, do you believe

that? Does that make any sense at all? That a fifteen-year career sergeant would just up and decide to quit and come home and look out for granny? I'm guessing he wore out his welcome with the U.S. Army and found himself booted out the door."

Sandi opened her mouth to defend him, but then realized she didn't have a comeback. Nothing she could prove anyway. Just a gut feeling. And if she shared that, LeAnne would be all over her for "going soft" on Bryce.

"See?" LeAnne continued. "Honey, do yourself a favor and stay away from that man. I'm not saying he can't be a charmer, can't make you go all tingly inside. Fill your head with stardust. I'm sure he has that down to a fine art."

Her mother-in-law leaned forward. "But is that really what you want in your and Gina's life? A man with no substance? You always act like your faith is such a big part of your life. I know it was in Keith's, little good it did him. But surely even bottle-thick, rose-colored glasses can't blind you to the fact that Bryce never has and never will share that part of your life."

"He says he gave his life to God after Keith died."

"Oh, please. He certainly knows which chords to strum to capture your attention, doesn't he?"

That's not what was happening—was it?

"I'm quite happy where I am in my life right now. Things are going well at the school. Gina's thriving. I'm in no hurry to add a man into the mix."

No *hurry*. But…

"I'm relieved to hear that. When I saw him over here that night we had ice cream, heard you'd gone to the equine center grand opening with him—"

"I already told you I didn't go *with* him."

LeAnne waved her away. "Sweetheart, Keith isn't here to look out for you. To protect you from the likes of men like Bryce. I'm not trying to cheat you out of a chance at happiness. I'd be delighted if a few years down the road—with the right man—you're ready for another relationship. Ready to have more kids—even if they won't be Keith's."

Sandi drew in a sharp breath, the piercing reminder of her final words to her husband echoing through her mind. No, she'd never have more children. She didn't deserve them.

LeAnne reached across the table to give her hand a reassuring pat. "I have your best interests at heart, Sandi. Yours and Gina's. And the bottom line is that Bryce Harding isn't in your best interests. Be on your guard."

Chapter Seventeen

"I told her, Grandma," Bryce said as he pushed the cart down the aisle of Wyatt's Grocery on Saturday morning. "About the remodeling plans for downstairs."

Grandma looked up from where she'd been reading the recipe on the back of a tomato sauce can. "How'd she take it?"

"Pretty good." If you could call losing her spark and spunk pretty good. But no way was he telling Grandma he'd broadsided Sandi with his announcement. She didn't need to get down about it just because her grandson couldn't come up with a better solution to the situation. Dealing with one dejected female was bad enough. He didn't need to make it two.

"I'm relieved to hear that. The museum's a big part of her life since her husband passed on. So what's the plan?"

"I told her the remodel won't start right away. Maybe spring, so there's no hurry for them to get out. Told her I'd help her look for another place to relocate."

"Did you, now?" Her eyes twinkled as she placed the can in the cart. "You poor thing. Having to spend extra time with that sorry-looking woman."

He gripped the cart's handle as he envisioned Sandi that day at the lake. How the breeze ruffled her hair. How she gazed at the clouds in wonder. "It's strictly business. Trying to do the right thing. I feel bad about moving the historical society out. But it can't be helped."

"Well, then, just make sure you don't enjoy yourself too much in her company." She winked. "You know, seeing as it's strictly business."

"It is."

She didn't look as though she bought a word of it. But he wasn't going to admit he'd already picked up a stack of real estate guides from the chamber of commerce and had gone online to check out properties. Not a whole lot available for what Sandi was probably looking for at a price the society could afford. He didn't see her setting up shop in a strip mall for long. She'd want more—what was it called on that home and garden TV program? Oh, yeah. Ambiance. Atmosphere. Character. But he'd spied a few possibilities.

So what if he was looking forward to helping out? That didn't mean he was taking a too-personal interest in her. It was the least he could do. Not only because he was the driving force behind the museum relocation, but because she was his best buddy's widow. He owed Keith, right?

Keith would have done the same had it been Bryce,

not Keith, who'd been killed in action and left a beautiful, vulnerable young woman behind. One with captivating eyes, a more than pleasing figure and a very appealing mouth. A tenderhearted spirit. Caring mom. Woman of faith. A female any red-blooded man might take a second—or third or fourth—look at if her somewhat bossy nature didn't send him hightailing it for the hills.

Although she seemed to be mellowing a bit.

Or was *he* mellowing?

"You've not heard a single thing I've said," Grandma scolded, but her eyes held a shrewd look he didn't much care for. Sometimes it was as if that woman had X-ray vision into the workings of his brain. Scary.

He cleared his throat. "Sorry. What did you say?"

"Do you want the pork steaks or chicken? You said you wanted to cook out tonight."

"Mmm. Chicken."

"My thoughts exactly."

He eyed her. "What's that supposed to mean?"

"Just never thought," she said, eyes dancing, "that I'd see the day my grandson chickened out when it came to staking a claim on a woman he had an interest in."

"I don't have an interest in Sandi."

She gave him a "look" that called him a liar. Right to his face.

"I told you before, our connection to each other is Keith. That's all it is."

Grandma Mae gasped, her eyes widening as she threw her arms in a protective gesture over her head. Ducked. Swiveled to look above the shelves. Toward the ceiling.

"What is it?" He braced himself, trying to spot what alarmed her. What he had to defend her from.

She lowered her hands, straightened up. Bestowed a matter-of-fact nod. "Flying pigs."

He cracked a smile. "I'm telling you, Grandma—"

"Believe what you want to believe if it makes you feel better, young man." She lowered her voice. "But don't tell me it's my imagination that you have, as the kids say, the hots for Sandi Bradshaw. Why can't you admit you've taken a liking to the girl? No shame in that, is there?"

She pinned him with an amused gaze. Made him squirm.

"No. I guess not."

"Well, then? Are you going to see her today?"

He gave the cart a push. "No. I'm going fishing."

And the sooner the better.

Congratulations, Mrs. Bradshaw. I hope you're proud of yourself for miring our beloved historical society in this mess.

Sharlene's scornful voice echoed in Sandi's head as she pressed her foot to the gas pedal. Hands shaking on the steering wheel and stomach churning, she sped from the Saturday-morning meeting where she'd delivered the news of the building's fate.

Why'd you let her go off on me like that, God? Let her humiliate me.

Cate Landreth hadn't been present to stand up for her this time. Or Earl. Everyone else had sat dumbstruck when Sharlene started her rant, calling for the society president's removal from office before elections this autumn.

Still numb from the dismal turn of events clouding the museum's future, Sandi hadn't the willpower to defend herself. She'd sat there like all the others. Withdrawing into herself and bearing the staggering punch of every verbal blow. When at long last Sharlene had paused to take a breath, she'd found the strength to rise to her feet. Looked Sharlene in the eye. Then gathered her purse and jacket and headed out the door.

She'd never go back. Ever.

Her hands tightened on the steering wheel. She wouldn't cry. She wouldn't.

God, why is this happening? And why now?

She'd been so close to achieving her dream for Keith. Had already spoken confidentially with interior designer Kara Dixon about upgrading the space. Display cases were needed. Lighting. The damaged flooring should be replaced. Walls painted. All along she knew if she could foot the bill for most of it, work her tail off to win the society members' admiration, it would be a natural next step to dedicate the room to her husband.

Or that's what she'd thought until Bryce's bombshell.

And then this.

Sharlene's words hammered. Irresponsible. Mismanagement. Negligence. Poor judgment. She'd ripped her to shreds.

But where had her defenders been?

Did they just sit there because they were cowed by the former president—or buying into everything she said? Had all this time they let her think she was doing a good job? Led her to believe she'd won their support, friendship and confidence when all the while they had their doubts?

Sandi slammed a fist against the steering wheel.

How could they do this to her?

And how could You let it happen, Lord? What did I do to deserve this?

Chin trembling, she blinked rapidly, fighting tears as the answer stepped boldly into her conscience.

Keith. What she'd done to Keith.

A sob racked from the very depths of her being.

Keith.

She did deserve this. All of it.

She pressed the gas pedal harder as she neared the outskirts of town, and the car leaped forward. Maybe she'd keep driving. It didn't matter where. If she had Gina with her maybe she'd drive right on out of this place and never look back. It wasn't like her to turn tail and run. But she was tired. So tired of trying to keep everyone around her happy. Of trying to prove herself valuable. Worthy.

But why was all this happening *now*?

The image of Bryce's handsome face rose up.

It was *his* fault.

If he hadn't come back, his grandma would have gotten a ground-floor apartment elsewhere and continued to rent the museum to the society. But oh, no, the Incredible Hulk had to move in with plans of his own.

Sailing down the road, faster and faster, she longed to put the gas pedal to the floor. But she couldn't go far. Not without telling someone. Gina, spending the day with the pastor's kids, might need her.

Flying around a sharp corner between the towering ponderosas, she spied Casey Lake off to her right, stretching serenely across the treed terrain. Easing up on the gas, she braked to turn onto the graveled road winding its way among the pines to the picnic ramadas. Boat ramps. Heartbeat slowing and still determined not to cry, she found a spot in one of the parking lots. Shaky fingers opened the trunk and locked her purse inside.

A walk. A long walk. That's what she needed. Time alone with God.

She'd barely reached the wooded trail when she heard someone call her name.

No. Not now. Not him.

She picked up the pace, pretending she didn't hear.

"Sandi!" the voice called again, accompanied by the sound of running footsteps, rock and gravel crunching under his swift feet. She'd never outrun Bryce.

Drawing a deep breath to regain her composure, she pasted on a smile. Turned to where Bryce jogged toward her, fishing pole and tackle box in hand, his cowboy hat tilted jauntily on his handsome head. She'd been so preoccupied, she hadn't noticed his old SUV in the lot.

"Hello, Bryce." Could she sound any less enthusiastic?

"Hello, yourself." He came to a halt in front of her, not even breathing hard and looking better than any man had a right to look in a T-shirt and worn jeans. He tightened his grip on the tackle box, a smile broadening as if he was genuinely happy to see her. "What are you doing out here on a Saturday morning? I don't see any fishing gear."

He glanced around her as if looking for bait and tackle. Then winked.

"Going for a walk."

His dark eyes studied her a little too sharply. *What did he see? Red eyes? Mussed-up hair? Sniffling nose?* "Would you like some company?"

What she'd like is for a hole in the ground to open up and swallow her. Now.

She shrugged noncommittally, suppressing a still-smoldering anger toward him. She'd like nothing better than to get her hands around that muscled neck of his and— "Your choice. Just don't expect me to be *good* company."

Maybe he'd take the hint.

"Why's that?"

She shrugged. "Just not a good day."

"No? Maybe I can do something to turn that around."

With an almost tangible excitement, he tucked his fishing gear out of sight at the base of a nearby ponderosa. Then moved in beside her as she turned again toward the path. "I think I've found a few museum options for you to take a look at."

Interest sparked. Then dimmed. It didn't much matter if he'd come up with cheap rent for the Smithsonian itself. Her days with the historical society were over.

"Thanks." She kept her eye on the trail. "But you should probably share that information with Sharlene Odel."

"She's heading up the relocation committee or something?"

"Or something."

His warm hand on her arm drew her to a halt. "What aren't you telling me?"

She looked into his troubled gaze. "I'm being ousted as the historical society president."

His expression darkened. "What? Why?"

She tilted her head and looked pointedly up at him. Bryce Harding. The instigator of all her recent troubles.

His eyes widened momentarily, then his brows lowered. "Because of me? Because of what I need to do to the house for Grandma Mae?"

"Ah, but you see, you wouldn't be doing that if it weren't for me. You know, because of my incompetence. My poor leadership skills. Had I been a capable president, I'd have foreseen this turn of events. Would have cleverly negotiated. Changed your mind."

He snorted. "Then they don't know me."

"Tell them that."

"Maybe I will."

She shook her head with a bone-deep weariness. "Don't bother. They've made up their minds."

"They? The whole board? All the members? Or just Sharlene?"

"When she lit into me this morning, let's just say no one voiced any objections."

He folded muscled arms across his chest. "Then there will be no lease renewal. So they'd better start packing, because they're out of there come July 31."

Her heart soared at the determination in his voice. Someone on her side. But would they run her out of town—him, too—if he pulled a stunt like that? Shar knew a lot of people. Hung out with the town's elite. Then again, would being run out of town be all that bad? If she couldn't present to LeAnne a veterans exhibit named in honor of her son, what would be the point in remaining in a place she'd never truly belonged?

"I appreciate your support, Bryce, but if Shar wants to run the historical society again, thinks she can do a better job of it than I can, then she's welcome to it."

"Nobody's going to treat you like that and get away with it."

"This is a war I won't win." She stepped away from

him to lean against the rough bark of a ponderosa, the last of her energy draining out of her.

He moved in closer, still looking disgruntled.

"Look, Sandi. I may be new at this God stuff, but don't you think He sometimes wants us to take a stand? Not just roll over and play dead? Let me set them straight. None of this is your fault."

She shook her head and stared at the uneven, pine-needled ground. She would *not* cry. "There's no point. I'm finally realizing I've lived in a make-believe world since Keith dropped me off in Canyon Springs seven years ago. I'd fooled myself into believing I'd become a part of the community. But I haven't. I'll always be an outsider."

"One person and her little clique doesn't make a whole town. Not by a long shot." He took another step and, to her surprise, gently cupped her face in his big, callused hands.

She drew a slow breath, mesmerized by the intensity in his eyes.

"It's going to be okay, Sandi." His soft words reassured. Then he leaned forward and kissed her forehead. A quick I'm-on-your-side kiss like she'd so often given Gina.

Nevertheless, her heart rate escalated as his gaze embraced hers for a long moment, something fierce and powerful and protective flickering through his eyes. A smiled tugged at his lips as he gazed down at her almost as if in wonderment.

"You know what?" He took a long, slow breath, his gaze never leaving hers.

She swallowed, her own breath labored. "What?"

"I'm going to kiss you, Sandi Bradshaw."

"I think you just did." She forced a teasing lilt into her soft words. But her heart beat faster.

"No, I mean *really* kiss you."

Her eyes widened and he chuckled.

"You heard me."

"Bryce—" This shouldn't be happening. She should pull away. Run even. But she stood as if paralyzed, relaxing into the touch of his hands still cradling her face.

Then he leaned in, lowering his head.

She closed her eyes. Parted her lips in anticipation. Waited for the moment his lips made contact with hers.

But they didn't.

Heart still laboring after an embarrassingly long moment, she opened one eye to peek.

He'd pulled back slightly, gazing at her with longing. "You're so beautiful, Sandi. So good. I have no right to kiss you."

He was debating this?

She placed her hand on his chest. Big guy. Strong. Solid.

Taking a ragged breath, she gazed up at him. She *wanted* him to kiss her. Wanted to kiss him back. Which was insane. This was the man who—

She gripped the front of his shirt, her gaze drowning in his. "Maybe you don't have the right. But don't let that stop you."

The surprise reflected in his eyes swiftly transformed to resolve. "I hope we don't regret this, Sandi."

Tugging on his shirtfront, she tossed caution to the wind, her voice husky. "Me, too."

He leaned in again, his mustache softly tickling as he gently pressed his lips to hers.

Chapter Eighteen

At long last, Bryce finally drew back, his heart almost pounding its way right out of his chest.

He'd just kissed Sandi Bradshaw.

Keith's wife.

And lightning hadn't struck him.

Or at least not the kind that literally knocked him off his feet and fried him to a crisp. No, not physically struck, but emotionally it was another story. When had he ever felt this way about a woman? Not just the physical attraction, but the rest of the package people always talked about. Where you wanted to scoop her into your arms and keep her by your side forever.

Sandi looked up at him, wide eyes searching his. He smoothed her hair with his hand. Soft. Silky. She smelled good, too. He squinted one eye and peered cautiously skyward with an exaggerated wariness. "Well, at least we didn't get hit by a bolt out of the blue."

"Speak for yourself, Sergeant."

So she felt it, too? Whoever would have thought?

He stared down at her, trying to read every nuance of her expression. "I have to confess something, Sandi."

Her dubious look said she wasn't sure she wanted to hear it, but he proceeded anyway. "I think I've been wanting to do that since the first day I ran into you at the Warehouse."

Her cheeks tinted a pretty shade of pink.

He chuckled. "Didn't figure it was a real good idea at the time, though. You know, considering."

"Yeah, considering." She tightened her grip on the front of his shirt. "I thought you probably wanted to strangle me."

"That, too."

She punched him playfully in the chest, but it felt like no more than a butterfly's nudge. He chuckled again and stroked her hair, still staring at her in amazement.

Sandi. He'd just kissed Sandi.

Wanting to do it again, he leaned in once more.

With a startled gasp she jerked away, her fearful gaze fixed on something behind him. He swung around, adrenaline pumping to take on whatever threatened her safety.

For a moment he wasn't sure what she'd seen. His eyes searched the perimeter of the lake for an elk. Bear. Mountain lion. Then came to rest on a small group of female hikers he hadn't noticed before, lounging under one of the pine-shaded picnic ramadas. He focused on one woman in particular who stared right at them.

Lightning had struck after all.

LeAnne Bradshaw.

"You have to listen to me," Sandi insisted an hour later, back at her trailer and clutching the cell phone to her ear. "Please, LeAnne, let me explain."

"There's nothing to explain. I saw it with my own eyes. You and that, that, Harding fellow in a lip-lock. Hands all over each other in broad daylight. Right in front of me and my friends. Friends who've met you before. Who recognized you. I don't know when I've been so humiliated."

"I'm sorry, but that's not what happened and not what you saw, LeAnne. It was very chaste and innocent."

"My land, Sandi. There's never been anything innocent about Bryce Harding. Surely Keith didn't keep you in the dark about him. About his background. His lifestyle."

"He's a changed man."

"I certainly saw evidence of that today, didn't I? Now he thinks he has a right to maul Keith's wife. And why would he think that, Sandi, unless you'd led him to believe it?"

"I didn't—"

Or did she? The flood of sensations she'd felt when Bryce's lips had touched hers washed through her again. She'd wanted him to kiss her. Had told him so.

"It started with not wearing your wedding ring a few years ago," her mother-in-law continued. "I told you that would lead to trouble, didn't I? It signals to men that you're a woman alone. Available. Looking."

She *was* a woman alone, wasn't she? For five long, guilt-ridden years. But she hadn't been "looking." Wasn't looking now.

Sandi paced the floor of her trailer. "The ring led to too many misunderstandings. Uncomfortable explanations when people assumed I was married. They'd ask about my husband, invite me *and my husband* to social events. Then they'd be embarrassed when I said I was a widow. It confused Gina, too, when she overheard those conversations."

"Nonsense."

"LeAnne—" Why wouldn't she listen? Why was she assuming the worst of her? Of Bryce? Making those sweet, too-brief moments out to be some ugly, dirty thing? "I was upset. He was comforting me."

"That was quite the comfort my friends and I saw."

"Please, just listen. I'm in the doghouse with the historical society members because we have to relocate. Bryce offered his support, promised to talk to them."

"I didn't see much talking going on. And I certainly don't understand how you could let that man touch you, let alone kiss you. Not after being married to my son. The finest young man on the face of the earth. How can you so quickly forget the father of your child? Toss him in the trash heap and take up with a man far his inferior?"

Sandi's attention focused on Keith's photo in the bookcase, the very blood in her veins turning to ice. "I haven't tossed my husband in any trash heap."

Her mother-in-law sighed. "I wouldn't say these things if I weren't concerned. Deeply concerned. A man like Bryce Harding can bring nothing but misery to you. To Gina. She's your priority, Sandi. Don't forget that."

"I haven't."

"Oh, honey, things were so good between us before this man came back to town." LeAnne's strident tone shifted to a more persuasive one. "Can't you see what he's doing to you? To us? Please don't let this man come between us, let him snatch away the friendship we've shared since Keith's passing. Bryce is using you, sweetheart. Open your eyes."

He hadn't seen her for days.

Not since LeAnne spied them at the lake and marched off with her friends, climbed into her big Cadillac and hit the gas. A stricken Sandi had pushed him away and hurried to her own vehicle with not even a glance in his direction.

Lousy way to end a kiss.

He pulled out his cell phone for at least the twentieth time that day alone, prepared to punch in Sandi's number. But what would he say? Besides, if she wanted to talk to him, wouldn't she call?

He pocketed it again, then put the empty stock truck in gear and backed it up to the loading dock of one of the outbuildings at the High Country Equine Center. Afternoon storm clouds gathered overhead and he could smell rain in the air. Feel a cool front moving in that would soon drop the temperatures from the upper eighties into the sixties.

Lightning flashed. Thunder rumbled. Wouldn't be long.

Inside the building where Trey stored hay apart from the stable area, he strode to a side room to dig out a pair of gloves. Some hay hooks. With Trey out of town, he'd promised Kara he'd transfer a load of bales to the main facility this afternoon.

He found the gloves easily enough. Now where'd those hay hooks go?

As he searched, his mind again drifted to Sandi. Couldn't help but smile. Yeah, he'd sure enough kissed her all right. Enjoyed it, too. Not to brag, but he thought she took some pleasure in it, as well. But leave it to Keith's mom to show up. Spook her off.

He didn't think it any coincidence, after seeing the look on her face when she spied her mother-in-law, that Sandi had kept herself scarce. Just as with her son, LeAnne had a direction she intended her daughter-in-law to go—and if Keith's mom had any say about it, Bryce would be abducted by aliens and held hostage for a few millennia. Keith asserted himself early on, shook off her controlling ways.

But how sturdy was Sandi's backbone?

What the kiss meant to her, if anything, he hadn't a clue. And on his own part, had that been Old Bryce sneaking out for a taste of a pretty woman? Or New Bryce, opening blinded eyes to a lady God wanted him to see in a different light?

If nothing else, he owed her an apology for his rampant misconceptions. His interference in her and Keith's courtship. Their marriage. Planting doubts. Pointing out her shortcomings. Determined not to allow his buddy to succumb to yet another controlling female.

Thunder shook the ground, sounding as if it meant business, and he renewed his efforts to locate the hay hooks. If he didn't get that load transferred before the storm broke, he'd be stuck here until it passed on by. Horses had to eat.

Ah. There they were. He snagged a pair of handled, foot-long curved-steel tools from the top shelf just as, without further prelude, the sky let loose, rain hammering the steel expanse over his head with a deafening roar.

Well, that sealed the deal.

He tossed the hooks and gloves to a nearby workbench and looked around for something with which to occupy himself.

"Kara!"

Over the pounding rain he heard the shriek. Quickly he stepped into the hay-filled main part of the building to investigate—just as a sopping-wet someone shot through the outside door and plowed into him.

He staggered, instinctively reaching out to steady the form while managing not to fall over a bucket on the floor behind him.

Sandi.

Her startled eyes met his, her sodden wetness soaking his shirtfront where she pressed against him. She pulled away, her face contorted with disgust.

At the cold, drenching rain, he hoped—not at him.

"I'm sorry." She shook her dripping hair as her expression transformed to one of apology. "I guess I wasn't looking where I was going. And now look at the mess I've made of you."

She brushed at the dark, spreading spots on his shirt, but he caught her hand. Eased it away.

"No problem. I've been wet before."

She slipped her hand from his, then stepped well away from him. Shook herself like some cute little hound dog, sending water droplets flying. Her gaze met his as he took in her eye-catching performance, and she laughed. Fluffed her hair.

"I must look like something a cat would drag in."

"Don't have a cat." He winked. "May have to get one."

Her face flushed as she concentrated on pulling her sweatshirt's wet fabric away from her skin. She finally unzipped and peeled out of it, revealing a still-dry camp shirt.

He took the fleece-lined jacket from her and spread it on the rung of a ladder which leaned against the wall.

"Where's Kara?" She rubbed her hands together, glancing around the interior of the metal-sided building. "Mike said he thought she'd come down here for a load of hay."

"She was late for a meeting. I said I'd take care of it."

"Oh."

An awkward silence yawned between them.

"Haven't seen you in a while," he ventured. "You off work this afternoon?"

"Yeah. Gina's at her grandma's, so I'm catching up on errands." She darted a look at him. "Got a letter from an attorney in Utah. An anonymous benefactor—a fan of the museum—wants to make regular substantial donations. Perfect timing to help with the rent."

"That's great."

"I suspect it's one of the Salt Lake ladies I met Memorial Day. They loved Canyon Springs and our museum, so I've asked the attorney to confirm that any donations are approved for a future location as well as the current one. We're looking at alternate properties."

"So everything's smoothed out with the historical society?" That would mean a load off his shoulders.

"For the time being. I learned that as soon as I was out the door that day, several of the members lined out Sharlene. Which took guts considering her family's standing in the community. Anyway, they begged me not to resign, so I'm back in—unless election day changes that."

"Glad to hear it," he said, even though Old Bryce might have enjoyed tossing Sharlene and her cohorts out on their fannies come the last day of July.

Lightning crackled, followed by an earthshaking rumble. Sandi turned to the open door. "Quite the storm."

"Sure is." He moved to her side, careful not to stand too close. She seemed ready to bolt if it weren't for the rain coming down in solid, windblown sheets.

"Smells good, doesn't it?" She gave him a quick, questioning glance.

"Sure does."

"I had no idea there were seasonal monsoons in Arizona until I moved here. This part of the country wasn't anything like I thought it would be. I always pictured Arizona more like the Sahara, only with saguaro cactus."

They stood for some moments, watching the rain. Listening to it echo on the roof. He scuffed a booted toe on the concrete floor and took a steadying breath. Well, guess there was no time like the present to say what he needed to say. No telling when he'd find another opportunity to get her alone.

Chapter Nineteen

"I owe you an apology, Sandi."

An uncertain look lit her eyes. "You don't need to apologize, Bryce."

"I think I do."

"No, it was my fault. I accept part of the responsibility anyway." She met his gaze full-on for the first time since her arrival. "I wanted to kiss you, too."

Heart swelling, he gave her a lopsided grin. "That's good to know—but that's not what I was talking about."

The color in her face deepened with the realization of what she'd unnecessarily confessed to. "Oh."

"I'm talking about you and Keith. About how I tried to talk him out of marrying you. How I thought you were the bossiest little gal I'd ever come across. I was dead certain you'd make my buddy's life miserable."

Something flickered in her expression. Hurt? Guilt? Regret? With a jolt of alarm he sensed her distancing herself from him.

He shouldn't have mentioned Keith. Shouldn't have tried to apologize right now. Not when they were still trying to come to terms with their relationship. That kiss. Why couldn't he have left it alone for another day or two? Or twenty?

"But I was wrong about you, Sandi." He reached for her hand and gave it a gentle squeeze as if physical contact could draw her back. "I apologize. And I want to ask your forgiveness."

"Bryce—"

"I'll understand if you can't give it, but God's been doing things in my life in the years since Keith's death. I have a lot of regrets in my life, Sandi. Lots of things I wish I'd done differently. But I vowed when God found me that I'd put the past in the past and leave it there. Do my best to live a life I wouldn't regret."

"So that's what the shirt means?"

"Right." He gave her hand another squeeze. "But this is one regret that won't go away now that I've come to know you. Now that you're not just some other guy's woman on the other end of the phone. There's a lot I didn't understand back then. Things I understand better now. Like who you really are... and why Keith thought he was the luckiest man in the world."

Sandi swallowed, her mind racing. After all these years he was apologizing. But he shouldn't be. He'd been right about her all along. She *had* been immature. Needy. And yes, too controlling, too demanding at times. Too given to putting her foot down and being unwilling to budge.

"You don't need to apologize, Bryce."

"I do. I'm responsible for planting all sorts of doubts in Keith's head, right from the get-go when he first received your Dear Soldier letter. I can be a suspicious sort, Sandi. Life's taught me to be that way around women—except my grandma. You and Keith got caught in the fallout."

"But he didn't listen to you. He married me anyway."

Shouldn't have, but he did.

"Stubborn cuss, wasn't he?" Bryce shot her a teasing look, then sobered. "But he delayed responding to your letter because of my warnings. Delayed meeting you. Delayed getting engaged. All because of me. I'm sorry for that."

She nodded, staring down at their clasped hands.

"After you got married, I had no idea you wanted out of Canyon Springs because you were scared to be here alone. Refused to go fishing because you can't swim well. I just thought—well, no point in going into that."

He'd thought she was bossing her man.

And she had been.

"I'm no saint, Bryce." She nibbled at her lower lip. "I resented being stuck in Canyon Springs. I *did* want out of here, and I didn't go about voicing my determination the right way."

"But can you forgive me?"

"I can. And I do."

He ducked his head slightly. "Can we set aside our misconceptions of each other? Start over? Clean slate?"

She nodded, her smile tremulous.

He drew in a deep breath. "Now about that kiss."

Her startled eyes met his.

"You see, Sandi—" His voice, now husky, barely registered over the pounding of the rain. "That's concerned me. You know, you being Keith's wife. Feels like I'm crowding in on his territory. Never been one to do that to a buddy."

"I don't think Keith would object to our being friends."

He squinted one eye. "But what if we wanted to be more than friends?"

She stepped away from him, pulling her hands free and tucking them behind her back.

"Both of us are hurting, Bryce," she said gently. "Drawn together by our shared loss. But I don't think either of us wants to pursue something we'd later come to regret."

His mouth twisted as he gazed out the door at the slanting rain. After a long moment he cast a fleeting look at the ground, then back at her. Disappointment—in her—etched in his eyes.

"LeAnne got to you, didn't she?"

Her heart jerked. "What do you mean?"

"You know what I mean." His words came quietly

enough, but they were edged with resolve. "Did she make you rehearse those touching words of rejection, so you'd get it right? Don't let Keith's mom do to you what she tried to do to him."

She lifted her chin. "I'm not."

"Then explain the look I saw on your face when you spied her at the lake. Like a criminal caught in the act. Sirens wailing. Nowhere to run."

He stepped forward, crowding her, but there was no place for her to escape except into the downpour.

"I admit, Sandi, there was a time when Keith, too, would have warned you away from a man like me. He'd have been right to do it. But God's cleaning me up. That's the reason, the only reason, I can stand here with the confidence to ask if you'd consider me as more than a friend."

He reached out to gently cup the side of her face in one hand. "Don't let LeAnne put words in your mouth. Steal the feelings from your heart."

She pressed the side of her face into his hand. Closed her eyes as waves of something she hadn't felt in a long time washed over her. Warming. Touching deep inside the core of her, a fragile place she'd kept under lock and key for five long years.

Love?

"She never wanted me to marry Keith." She opened her eyes to see Bryce still gazing down at her, his expression filled with tenderness.

"It doesn't surprise me. The two of us really messed up her plans for him, didn't we?"

His thumb grazed her cheek.

"LeAnne is very special to me, Bryce."

"I know that."

"When Keith died she came to Canyon Springs almost every weekend, even in the winter, to make sure I wouldn't be alone. Gave me breaks from the demands of a little one. She's good to me. Very good."

"I'm not saying she isn't. It's just that she has her life to live and you have yours."

She pressed her lips together. "LeAnne doesn't believe you've changed."

"She wouldn't. But what about you? What do you believe?"

His thumb again caressed her cheek, distracting her. "I know God can do...amazing stuff."

"Stuff?" His gaze intensified, amusement glinting.

"I know Keith was proud to be your friend. I know he prayed for you. And I believe God answers prayers." She closed her eyes again, shutting him out. She couldn't think straight with him looking at her like that, as though he could read her with ease. "I just don't want us making a mistake."

"Meaning you don't want me to kiss you again?"

With a gasp, her eyes flew open.

"Let's hear you deny it, Sandi," he teased. "Hear you tell me you don't want to be kissed."

He was daring her?

She pinned him with a scowl. "I don't want..."

He raised a brow, stepped in closer.

"You..."

Slipping his other hand beneath her hair, fingers caressed the back of her neck.

"To kiss…"

"…me."

The breathless word came a millisecond before his lips met hers. To his delight, she melted right into him, arms slipping around his neck as though she'd come home following a too-long journey. He'd hoped it wouldn't take much convincing to coax a second kiss out of her, but this was more than he could have dreamed.

He drew her closer, feeling the warmth of her waist under his palms, drinking in her vanilla scent. Never wanting to let her go.

Was this really happening, or was he dreaming it?

When at last he reluctantly drew back, he leaned his forehead against hers. "This is getting to be a habit."

"A nice one."

He nodded.

"So," he whispered. "Where do we go from here?"

She pulled back slightly to study him, her gaze still smoldering, flickering with the same awe, the disbelief, he felt himself. "Where do you *want* to go?"

He wanted to wake up each morning with her by his side. Come home every night to her smile, even if he had to put out the garbage and fix his own dinner and find his own slippers. He still didn't understand it. Why God was letting a no-good bum like him slip into the blessings a guy like Keith deserved. But he wouldn't look a gift horse in the mouth.

Or question the Almighty.

He wasn't that dumb.

"I'd like to see where God takes this. Us."

"Me, too."

The sun split through a crack in the clouds, heralding the afternoon thundershower coming to an end. The same look of wonder he felt dawned on Sandi's pretty face, and he reluctantly released her. Then reached for her hand.

"What do you say I get this load of hay moved and you follow me over to Grandma's?" No way was he going to let her out of his sight for long. "I promised her I'd grill dinner tonight. And you're invited."

"Won't she be surprised if I show up?"

"Doubtful."

Within thirty minutes, he'd transferred the hay and they headed home, him often glancing up in the SUV's rearview mirror just to make sure he hadn't made the whole afternoon up. But no, there she was, right behind him. Was it his imagination, or did the flowers surrounding the museum property seem brighter? The sky a deeper blue?

She pulled up behind him in the driveway, but before she could get out he was already at her door, smiling, holding it open. Feeling every bit like a kid bringing home his first puppy. Grandma was gonna dance with delight.

He clasped Sandi's hand in his, then sniffed the air. "Do you smell something? Smoke?"

She nodded. Looking up, he glimpsed a wraithlike haze floating through the ponderosa branches above their heads.

A violent tremor coursed through his body. Terror such as he'd never before felt, not even in combat.

Dropping Sandi's hand, he raced for the back of the house. Rounded the corner. Smoke billowed out an upstairs window.

Please, God, no.

"Call 911," he shouted. And headed for the stairs.

Chapter Twenty

A cup of coffee halfway to her lips, Sandi stared at the front-page headlines of the weekly paper Cate had just dropped on the Kit's Lodge tabletop in front of her.

ELECTRIAL FIRE INJURES LOCAL WOMAN.

And below that, a large photo taken outside the museum—a shot of paramedics gathered around a disgruntled-looking Mae sitting on a stretcher in the back end of an ambulance. The wide-angle lens captured Bryce and Sandi looking on—his arm firmly around her waist and her head on his shoulder, her hand pressed to the broad expanse of his chest.

Oh, no.

"Told you you'd made the news, didn't I?" Cate laughed with delight. "Regular celebrity."

"I didn't know you and Bryce Harding were an item," elderly waitress Sue Brown observed, peering over her shoulder. "I remember him when he was a towheaded kid. Know his grandma, too. My, my, but he turned out to be a fine-lookin' fellow."

"That's what I've been telling Sandi." Cate clucked her tongue. "But she's dragging her feet."

Was it her imagination or had half the female restaurant patrons turned to look at her, eager to get a gander at the woman who'd made the news wrapped in the arms of one of Canyon Springs's most eligible bachelors?

"We're just friends." What a liar she was.

Cate rolled her eyes. "Honey, get a clue. A man like that ain't made for being just friends."

"It's okay to have a male friend," Sue reassured as she cut a quelling look at Cate and refilled Sandi's coffee cup. "Being friends is a good place to start."

Cate scoffed. "Being friends is a good place to let the competition edge in."

"Uh, Cate," Sandi whispered. "Would you lower your voice please?"

"There's no call to be embarrassed, Sandi. Everybody knows you've been on your own for a long time. Are in need of a man. Whole town will be tickled pink, just you wait and see."

"Why are we all going to be tickled pink?" Meg Diaz maneuvered around Cate and a departing Sue to slip into the booth seat across from Sandi. She smiled uncertainly at their gossipy coworker.

Cate snatched up the newspaper and dropped it in front of Meg. "Would you look at that? Sandi's finally found herself a man."

Meg glanced at the paper, then at Sandi, her words guarded. "He's a really nice guy."

"Nice don't say the half of it." Cate winked. "If you know what I mean."

Meg folded the paper and handed it back to Cate. "Is that your daughter I saw waiting in a car outside?"

Cate slapped her forehead. "In all the excitement over Sandi, I forgot. Promised to take my girl shopping in Show Low after I stopped off for a box of fresh-baked cinnamon rolls. Guess I'd better get going."

She fixed an eye on Sandi. "And keep me posted, little lady, on any developments with you know who. We may get to keep the museum after all."

Laughing, she dropped the paper back on the table and headed off to get her cinnamon rolls.

Sandi dropped her face into her hands. Mortified. "I could kill that photographer."

"Definitely one of the drawbacks to a small town."

Straightening, Sandi gave a quick glance around the room to ensure everyone was minding their own business again, then reached for her coffee cup. Caught Meg smiling at her.

"What?"

"Well?" Her friend leaned forward, her eyes bright and voice low. "Are you going to keep me in suspense? What's going on with you and Mr. Muscle? If that photo is any indication, looks like things have heated up a notch since our picnic."

"You might say that." Face warming, Sandi couldn't contain a smile. "He wants to be more than friends."

"And?"

"So do I."

Meg's eyes widened. "Are you serious?"

She nodded, and Meg let out a little squeal.

"I'm so excited for you. You two make such a cute couple." She pursed her lips, thought a moment. "Okay, maybe not quite as cute of a couple as you'd make with my big brother, Rob, but cute nevertheless."

"Ha, ha. Bryce is meeting me for breakfast—Gina's at her grandma's. What are *you* doing here?"

"The same thing Cate was. Picking up cinnamon rolls for my morning Bible study group." Meg's eyes brightened as she looked over Sandi's shoulder toward the door. "Won't be staying long, though. Looks like, much to the disappointment of every single woman in town, you're about to have company."

Spirits rising in anticipation, Sandi turned.

She watched as Bryce wove his way among the tables, pausing occasionally while someone inquired about his grandma. Pointed out the photo in the paper. Punched him playfully in the shoulder. Gave him a thumbs-up.

No, there was nothing quite like a small town.

When he finally arrived, he nodded a greeting to Meg and slid into the seat beside Sandi.

"Well, it was great seeing you this morning, Sandi." Meg slipped out of the booth. "You, too, Bryce."

"Hey," he protested, "don't let me chase you off."

"Wouldn't dream of it." But Meg didn't linger. "Ciao."

Sandi cautiously turned to the big man next to her. What did he think of the photo of them plastered across the front page? "How's Mae this morning?"

"Madder than a caged coyote."

"Mad? Why?" She'd visited her last night at Pine Country Care, and she'd seemed tired but not angry.

He shook his head. "Guess."

Because of the photo in the paper. The two of them fastened to each other tighter than Velcro. It probably came as a shock to see her grandson publicly seeking solace in the arms of a woman, even one she knew.

"Because she fell down the stairs trying to get away from the fire?" she suggested. "Rebroke her ankle?"

Bryce grunted. "No. Because she made the front-page news in her oldest, most hated housedress. The one with the big, splotchy blue flowers."

Sandi put her hand to her mouth to squelch a laugh, relief washing through her. "Poor Mae."

"Believe me, she is one unhappy woman this morning. Rolled me right out of bed with her call, demanding I sue the paper."

"Maybe we both should."

"You mean because of that?" Frowning, he tapped their intertwined image on the paper in front of him. "Wouldn't do any good. The whole town's already read that thing from front to back like it's *USA TODAY* or something."

Expression troubled, he picked up the breakfast menu. Flipped through it without reading. Uneasily, she ran a playful finger along his biceps, astonished, as always, at the rock solidness of his arms.

"I saw you getting teased when you walked in here."

He tossed the menu back on the table.

"We're today's hot news, babe. Splashed across the front page like Hollywood tabloid celebrities." He cut her a probing look. "How do you feel about that?"

Sensing irritation in his words, she spoke with caution. "Kind of embarrassed, I suppose. You know, everyone knowing our business. I feel like a bug being examined under a microscope."

He picked up the menu again. Toyed with it a moment. "Are you thinking it might be a good idea to put a little distance between us? Until things die down, I mean?"

A queasy sense of foreboding rolled in her stomach.

"Like how much distance?" she managed to get out, teasingly eyeing the few inches that separated them in the booth. He'd been all for kissy-face-close just a few days ago. Ready to explore where God might take them. But now that his interest in her had been made public…?

He tossed the menu down again and clasped his hands on the table. "I don't know. Maybe enough to quell the wagging tongues. I know you're concerned about your reputation—about mine—this being such a small town and all."

An invisible fist slugged her in the stomach.

She might throw up.

He was having second thoughts. Backing out. Dumping her right here at Kit's Lodge in front of God and everybody.

She smiled. Stiffly. And removed her hand from his arm. "Whatever."

He raised a questioning brow. "You're good with that?"

She shrugged. Swallowed. Aware that at least half the room covertly watched them. The other half openly.

"Well, looky here." Bella Sanchez, a woman Sandi recognized as a customer from the Warehouse, paused at their table to beam at them. "If it isn't the two love-birds."

Bryce leaned back in the booth, his smile looking forced.

"So glad to see you're dating again, Sandi. I've worried so much about you. Prayed for you. You know, since Keith's passing." She winked at Bryce. "You take good care of this lady, you hear me?"

"Yes, ma'am."

Bella nodded, satisfied, and moved on.

Bryce placed his forearms on the table and clasped his hands, not looking at her. Cleared his throat. "I need to get going. Sorry I can't stay for breakfast. Trey asked me to help with some roping stock this morning while he's gone."

She nodded.

He frowned, studying her closely. "Everything okay?"

"Mmm-hmm."

"All right then." He slid out of the booth, leaned over and kissed the top of her head. "Take care, Sandi. See you around."

She gave him her brightest smile, conscious of prying eyes.

See you around. Not I'll see you later. Not even I'll give you a call. See you around.

She watched him weave his way back to the entrance. T-shirt tight across his broad-shouldered back. A muscled arm reaching out for a passing handshake. A strong hand securing his straw hat on his head.

Then he disappeared out the door.

And out of her life.

He'd been gut-punched in a fistfight before, but it didn't hold a candle to what he'd gone through yesterday. Was still going through. He had no doubt, from the look on Sandi's face when he sat down with her at Kit's, that she was dismayed by that photo in the paper. Of being seen with him, cuddled in his arms for the whole town to gawk at.

He shut and fastened the gate on a dozen calves he'd unloaded into the corral, then strode toward his SUV. Didn't fancy getting caught in the approaching afternoon monsoon.

Sandi's reaction hadn't come as any surprise. And

to be honest, why shouldn't she be concerned about it? About a splotch on a previously spotless reputation she'd fought long and hard to maintain. About the dirty assumptions people might make about the two of them together.

Yes, he was New Bryce now. He'd changed significantly in the past few years, but few here knew it. Wasn't like he wore a sign around his neck. He hadn't been back long enough for word to get around. Except for escorting his grandma to church, he hadn't exactly been vocal about it. Churchgoing didn't prove anything to most hereabouts anyway. When he was a teen everybody knew Old Man Addison had a lady love on the side, but he never missed a Sunday service. So nobody would pay his own Sunday appearances much mind, either.

Sure, maybe some noticed he no longer camped down at the Timbertop Bar as he used to when on leave and Grandma had gone to bed. Didn't hang out at a neighboring town honky-tonk on Saturday nights, making sure the local gals had a good time.

He kicked at a rock. Sent it sailing.

Grandma. If he'd have been home, this never would have happened to her. She'd wakened from a nap to find the apartment filling with smoke from an outlet in the bathroom. The new detector he'd installed last winter, recently tested, had apparently malfunctioned. She'd panicked, headed for the inside staircase. Slipped. Tumbled.

He'd never forget finding her near the bottom of the

stairs. Her arm flung out as if to break her fall, her body twisted in an unnatural position. All because he'd let himself get delayed with wooing Sandi. Not taking care of business.

Grandma didn't break her neck, though. Relatively minor injuries. That's what counted. He jerked the SUV's door open.

Some grandson he'd turned out to be.

Climbing into his vehicle, he tossed his hat and gloves onto the seat beside him. Then stared out the window to watch the pastured horses tearing at the fodder along the fence line, seemingly oblivious of the rumbling thunder. They'd seek shelter under the lean-to if so inclined. Then his gaze shifted to the hay-storage building, where only a few days ago it looked as if God was opening doors.

Doors to a future with Sandi.

He should have known better. LeAnne had done her dirty work well.

When he'd offered Sandi a way out, asked if she wanted to put some distance between them for a while, she didn't voice any objections. Didn't ask him why. Just kind of shrugged. Said "whatever." Basically jumped on it like a cat on a cricket while feigning in-difference.

Lightning flashed as he rammed the key into the ignition. Started the vehicle. Put it in gear. He might be dense at times, but he could see the handwriting on the wall. Looked as if New Bryce needed lessons on hearing the voice of God when it came to his love life.

* * *

"When were you going to get around to telling me, Bryce?" Sandi planted herself in front of him, hands on her hips, as he pounded the For Sale by Owner sign in the rocked area between the sidewalk and the street.

How dare he not even warn her?

"Figured I'd tell you next time I saw you."

"And when would that be?" He'd avoided her since that day at Kit's when he suggested they put some distance between them until hoopla from the photo died down. It hadn't. Almost every day for the remainder of the week she'd been teased and taunted about "that Harding fellow," sometimes even by people she hardly knew.

She could only hope he'd been similarly tortured. Would serve him right for not even calling her.

"I thought you planned to remodel in the spring. So we had plenty of time to find another location. But you're selling it now? Not remodeling?"

"The lease is up the last day of July. You haven't signed the new one." Bryce bumped his hat up on his forehead and waved toward the museum. "I don't want Grandma in that old place. Faulty wiring. Ancient plumbing. Had an inspector in, so I got an eye-opener. If I can get enough for it, get that firefighter job soon, I'll find us a nice modern ranch house. No way am I going to risk putting her back in this place. Don't want anyone else in there, either. So the museum's closed. I'll refund your money for the remaining weeks of the lease."

"Closed? You can't do that."

"Watch me. I already changed the locks."

She bent to tug at the sign, but it didn't budge. "Pull that thing out. You at least owe me a little time. Time to see if the historical society can pull together some backers. Purchase it outright."

"Sandi, the society can barely pay the rent. You told me that yourself. Where would they dig up enough money to buy it? I can't carry a loan. I need payment in full."

"I'll get it. Maybe that Utah donor will loan us the money, with interest, of course. And maybe we can qualify for a grant. You know, for an historic home. So we can fix it up."

"How long will it take you to find all that out?"

"I don't know about the grant. But I'll call the law firm today. Maybe I can get an answer within a week. Maybe two."

He folded his arms, a frown forming. "I don't know…"

"Come on, Bryce. It's the least you can do. You owe me."

"How do you figure that?"

"Because if it wasn't for you, your grandma would have moved to a ground-floor apartment after her first fall. Would have kept renting this place to us. We'd have had enough money set aside so I could push through a veterans exhibit. An exhibit that would honor my husband, among others."

He ran a hand along the back of his neck. "You're

not going to like this, but it seems to me you've put this place before everything else in your life. Before God."

She gasped. *How dare he?*

"When are you going to get it through that thick head of yours, Sandi, that getting some exhibit named after Keith isn't going to bring him back."

That's what he thought she was doing? Trying to resurrect Keith?

She stepped up to him, lifted her chin. "I'm appalled to hear that come out of your mouth, Sergeant Harding. You may not have wanted your best friend to marry me, but I never expected you to have any objections to my wanting to *honor* him."

How could she ever have let herself fall for a man like Bryce? Obstinate. Hard-hearted. Just like LeAnne warned.

Glaring at her, he reached down and jerked the sign out of the ground with ease. Tossed it at her feet.

"Okay. There you go. I'm giving you two weeks. That's it."

Chapter Twenty-One

He should have known it would be only a matter of time before she showed her true colors. Revealed the same bossy, controlling nature he'd suspected when she first latched on to Keith. Standing right on his own family's property a few days ago, she'd lined him out. Said he *owed* her.

He'd said a quick prayer. Gotten his temper under control. Agreed to give her two weeks before putting the place on the market. But no way would the historical society come up with the amount of money he was asking. He needed every dime and then some to swing a new place. He'd temporarily rented a one-bedroom, ground-floor apartment for himself and Grandma. Borrowed a cot so he could sleep in the living room. While smoke hadn't done significant damage downstairs, a filthy coating bonded to everything upstairs. And the whole house reeked.

Two weeks. He'd given Sandi two weeks, though little good it would do.

Yeah, he'd been harsh with her. Accusing her of venerating the museum. But it was the truth, wasn't it? Besides, he'd had it with her telling him what to do and how to do it. So what was he doing at two o'clock in the morning, glaring down at yellowed papers scattered across the apartment's kitchen table? Peering at the glowing computer screen teeming with his notes?

The past two nights he'd immersed himself in a crash course on Canyon Springs's history. Gathering names. Dates. Making connections between the earliest settlers from the 1920s—almost a hundred years ago—to their descendents still living in the community. Tracking down mailing addresses, emails and phone numbers on the web for those more far-flung.

Whether or not the effort would be a wasted one was anybody's guess. But now he had what he needed to get started.

Not surprising, he hadn't seen Sandi since the day he'd tossed the For Sale sign at her dainty little feet. Didn't expect to see her anytime soon, either. She hadn't been happy with him. She'd no doubt filled the intervening days scribbling away in that little red notebook of hers and rallying the historical society troops to find a way to buy Grandma's house.

Even though the effort was pointless, she'd kill herself trying. Which is why he'd sacrificed sleep to paw through old papers dug out of the museum storage room and study archived copies of the local newspaper that some faithful soul had scanned for online use.

He hated to admit it, but it was interesting stuff. In

his estimation, local history and family memoirs had never held a candle to national and world chronicles. But he was rethinking that. Seeing his own grandpa's name and Grandma Mae's crop up in his reading put a more personal spin on it. Made him wonder about where they'd come from, who their people were. His people.

He'd have to ask Gran.

But first he had a mountain of work ahead of him. Even if Sandi couldn't let go of Keith, put pleasing her mother-in-law above her feelings for him and wanted no part in his life…well, God help him, he loved her.

"Are you sure she won't reconsider?" Sandi tightened her grip on the cell phone. The donor's legal representative had called back several days later to inform her that not only would his client not be interested in providing a loan to the historical society, but there would be no further donations forthcoming. The museum, it had been determined after more careful investigation, was a poor investment.

"I'm sorry, Mrs. Bradshaw," the attorney concluded, "but I wish you and your historical society the best."

She shut off the phone and dropped down on the trailer's sofa, the last of her energy consumed. That was it. Her last hope. The museum as they knew it was no more.

"Not good news, I take it?" LeAnne asked from where she sat at the kitchen table. She'd dropped by to bring Gina a new book.

"No."

"So that Harding man is actually selling the museum right out from under you?" She tapped on the rim of her iced tea glass with a fingernail. "Like a man who claims to care for you—as you seemed to think he did a few weeks ago—would do something like that?"

"He's looking out for his grandma."

LeAnne sighed. "I think you're seeing him in a much too forgiving light."

"It's not his fault he has to sell the property or that I'm incapable of raising sufficient funds to buy it."

She'd tried. Really tried.

"You're still seeing him?" LeAnne's voice remained carefully neutral, no doubt not wanting to get into another on-edge conversation such as the one they'd found themselves in after she'd witnessed the lakeside kiss.

Sandi toyed with the trim on a throw pillow. "No. I'm not."

"Then let's put that episode behind us, shall we? Consider ourselves fortunate you didn't let yourself be taken in by him."

What could she say to that? She *had* been "taken in," her heart lured in by the handsome fisherman hook, line and sinker.

"We still have several weeks," LeAnne hurried on, her tone bright, "before you return to the classroom. Let's make the most of them. Make plans. You, me and Gina."

Sandi clutched the pillow to her chest, measuring her words carefully. "You know, LeAnne, you've been amazingly generous with your personal time, spending so much of it on Gina and me. I imagine you might enjoy a little more for yourself now."

"Nonsense." She smiled warmly. "I know you both need guidance, support, a little company in Keith's absence. That's what I'm here for."

"And we love you for it." Tracing her finger along the pillow's patterned fabric, Sandi returned her mother-in-law's smile. "But we're actually doing pretty well now."

"Takes time, doesn't it?"

"It has. But I imagine your friends have missed you at Friday-night gatherings. That you've missed them."

Please, Lord, let her not take this wrong.

LeAnne stilled, her gaze faltering. "I may be misunderstanding, but that almost sounds as if you'd rather not spend Friday nights with me."

"It's not that, it's just that it's been five years since we lost Keith. I know he'd want you—me—to move on with our lives."

LeAnne straightened, her spine rigid. "That's what you think I'm doing? Clinging to the past?"

Sandi's voice gentled. "It's what we both may be doing."

Hadn't Bryce made that clear? *The museum won't bring your husband back.* Harsh, unkind words. But she'd unwillingly been thinking about them. Praying about them. Was he right?

"I see." LeAnne stood. Carried her tea glass to the kitchen counter, where she remained gripping it in both hands. "I don't remember you feeling that way before Bryce Harding entered the picture."

"This isn't about Bryce. It's just that my eyes are opening to a lot of things this summer. About me."

"Then I imagine that newspaper photo was a wake-up call." The older woman's tone sharpened. "You can't hide secrets in a small town, can you?"

Sandi set the throw pillow aside. "We weren't having an affair, LeAnne. We care for each other, that's all."

At least she still cared for *him*.

"You still harbor an interest in him, don't you?" Her mother-in-law's gaze darkened. Voice escalated. Thank goodness Gina was outside playing. "Nothing good can come of pursuing a relationship with that man, and you know it."

Click. Click. Click.

Sandi gritted her teeth, but her words came quietly. Her tone teasing. "Will you please stop doing that?"

"Doing what?"

"That thing with your nails. Tapping."

LeAnne's face contorted and she slammed her glass into the sink, the sound of its shattering jerking Sandi to her feet.

"LeAnne—"

The woman held up a warning hand.

"You are such an ungrateful woman. So undeserving of my son. So quick to forget him and run after the same low-life man who dragged my Keith to his death. Do you have any idea what that photo did to me? You wrapped in each other's arms like there had never even been a Keith?" She slammed her fist on the counter. "I have not one single regret that I pulled those funds."

What was she talking about?

Bursting into tears, LeAnne covered her face with her hands. Sandi rushed to her, pulling the sobbing woman into her arms. She didn't resist, but collapsed into Sandi's embrace, clinging to her.

And Sandi cried, too.

Even half a decade after her husband's death, her heart bore testimony that there could never be another Keith. She hadn't deserved him then. Wasn't worthy now of another chance at a happily ever after. *He'd* never be given a second chance to pick out a more mature, supportive, understanding wife, now would he?

When at long last their sobs subsided and Sandi had guided her mother-in-law to the sofa, they sat together, dabbing at their eyes. All but emptying the tissue box on the coffee table.

"I'm so sorry, LeAnne."

"Me, too." She gripped Sandi's hand. "I broke your glass. A wedding present, wasn't it?"

Sandi nodded. They both laughed. Just a little, at the absurdity of her apology.

"Oh, Sandi, we loved him, didn't we?"

"We did. We do."

"I'm so sorry. About everything." The older woman sniffled, wiped her nose with a tissue. "But when I saw that photograph in the paper, I couldn't condone your behavior."

Sandi stiffened as realization dawned. "*You're* the anonymous donor. With the Utah attorney."

She nodded. "But I can be persuaded to reinstate my pledge. In fact, if you keep this unfortunate episode with Bryce in your past, I'll fund a new museum in its entirety."

Sandi stared at her, speechless.

"You can pick out a piece of property and build it from the ground up for all I care, sweetie. Just stop mooning over that man. I know this museum means so much to you. Let me do this. Please?"

A museum. A new one. Natural stone, set back in the pines. Climate controls and well-lit display cases. No more creaky floors and leaky windows. A veterans exhibit. Surely if LeAnne donated the building, the society would have to name it in memory of Keith, wouldn't they? Maybe the whole building.

The Keith Bradshaw Historical Museum.

LeAnne was right. There could be no future with Bryce. He'd already withdrawn emotionally even before their falling-out about the property's sale, about her commitment to the museum. Sadly, he was a man incapable of making a lasting commitment—a man who'd tried to keep Keith from making one.

No, she and Bryce would never share a future.

But she *could* have the museum.

"It's so easily done, Sandi. We can contact an architect, begin the design. Start looking for property."

"I'm overwhelmed, LeAnne. It's been my dream." She could honor her daughter's father. Make her mother-in-law proud. Make a lasting impact on the community. All she had to do was say yes and the dream was hers.

But in the stretching silence, gazing at Keith's mom, a still, small voice spoke to her heart.

Doubt flitted through her mother-in-law's eyes. "You won't let me do this for you? You won't give up that man? For the museum? For me?"

Understanding at last, Sandi placed a gentle hand on LeAnne's. "This isn't about Bryce, is it?"

"He's the only thing holding you back from your dream."

"Or," Sandi whispered, "is he holding *you* back from yours?"

Startled eyes met hers. "What do you mean?"

"You had dreams for Keith. And when Keith was gone, dreams for me. Gina."

"Of course. You're Keith's wife. Gina's my granddaughter. I love you both."

"But you blame Bryce for influencing him to join the army. To give up Harvard. The law firm. And now you're afraid Bryce will take Gina and me from you, as well."

A pained gasp slipped from her mother-in-laws's lips.

"We've become a family, haven't we, LeAnne? The

three of us. You. Me. Gina." Sandi tightened her grip on Keith's mom's hand. "Even if things had worked out with Bryce, that would never have changed. I wouldn't let it. And while I can't accept your offer for a new museum, I love you, LeAnne. And you will *always* be a part of my life."

Chapter Twenty-two

With a heavy heart, Sandi let herself through the museum gate and paused to take in her surroundings.

The weathered stone. A front porch needing fresh paint. Overgrown bushes demanding a trim. A pot of weary geraniums by the door. Had she seen it through eyes of love, so hadn't noticed those things? It was all she could do not to pull out her notebook and add new items to her checklist.

But what would be the point?

A week of nonstop campaigning had netted dozens of promises for financial support, but none that approached what the bank representative insisted would be required.

As she started up the stone steps, the front door opened and Bryce's imposing form filled the open space. With barely concealed excitement in his eyes, he stepped onto the porch—but she didn't see a For Sale sign clutched in his big hand, so at least he was showing a little sensitivity.

He motioned to the cozy area on the far end of the porch. "Want to have a seat? No point in confining ourselves inside on a nice day like this."

She followed his lead and seated herself on a padded wicker chair, leaving the hard-backed bench to him. Then she turned to him, forcing a tight smile. This was going to be harder than she thought it would be. "I guess you know why I invited you to meet me here."

His expression sobered. "Guessing."

"We can't swing it. Not the down payment. Not the monthly mortgage. Not the remodel."

"Your anonymous donor didn't come through?"

She shook her head.

"That donor turned out to be LeAnne." And not even presenting her with a veterans memorial as big as the state of Texas would have ever won her mother-in-law's approval. How had she been so blind?

He gave a low whistle. "Whoa. Didn't expect that. But she can't help out?"

Her memory flashed to LeAnne's proposed "deal" involving him. She wouldn't go into that. "No."

"I'm sorry."

But pity wasn't what she wanted from him. He looked so handsome sitting there across from her. Big, rough and tough on the outside—with a marshmallow center. What had gone so wrong between them, so quickly?

She gave a little shrug, as if it didn't matter. As if

nothing mattered. "You're free now to post your sign. Find a buyer."

Was it wrong to wish he couldn't find one?

Bryce leaned forward, forearms resting on his knees and hands clasped. "I already found one as a back-up plan."

Her stomach tightened as hope toppled.

His eyes searched hers, gauging her reaction, but his words squeezed out any foolish dregs of expectation that might remain in the bottom of her heart. Hope that he might negotiate. Bring down the price. But he'd known all along she didn't stand a chance of pulling it off. He'd humored her. That was all.

"When do we have to be out?"

"Grandma could transfer the property August 1. The potential buyer would like to get started on a remodel before month's end."

She hadn't expected it to happen so quickly. Where would they store everything? Relocate? She reached into her purse and pulled out her notebook. She had a lot to get done in the remaining days of July. "What's he plan to do with it? And please don't tell me Canyon Springs is getting yet another real estate office."

He chuckled. "No, he's a more civic-minded gentleman."

"Oh. Government offices?"

"Actually, a museum."

She frowned.

"Historical," he added, watching her closely.

"I...I don't understand. Who is this guy?"

"A descendant of the family who built this house. Lives in California. Made it big during the real estate boom, but got out before the crash. Now he wants to give back to the community his great-grandparents helped found, where his grandparents grew up."

She leaned forward.

"Are you kidding me?" The pitch of her voice rose right along with the hope within her. "He wants to remodel *this* place? Keep the museum *here?*"

"That's right. At no cost to the society"

She put her hand to her mouth. Tears forming. "How on earth—?"

Bryce's eyes twinkled.

"You." She laughed, still not taking it all in. "You did this, didn't you? Made it happen. But *how?* How did you find him?"

Rising to his feet, hands on his slim hips, he grinned down at her. "Let's just say I've gained a new respect for digging through the musty belongings of dead people. And the ties that bind U.S. Army alumni."

She stood, as well, her gaze never leaving his. "I think I want to hug you."

"I think I'm going to let you."

She laughed again and, stepping into his arms, pressed her cheek against his solid chest. Held him tight, just as he held her. She looked up. "Thank you, Bryce. I can't put into words how I feel. I can't believe you did this for me, even after changing your mind about us."

His gaze sharpened. "I never changed my mind about us. You did."

She pulled back slightly, shaking her head. "No, I didn't."

They stared at each other, eyes questioning.

Realization dawning.

Then he laughed—a laugh she loved—and tugged her into his arms again. "I asked you once before, Sandi, if we could be more than friends. What do you say now? Considering our track record, you may find it hard to believe, but I love you."

She tightened her hold on him. "I love you, too."

He glanced cautiously heavenward. "No lightning strikes. I think the Almighty approves. And Keith."

Her breath caught. And Keith.

You can forget about having any more children. At least with me, anyway.

She squeezed her eyes tightly shut.

"What's wrong? I'll fix it whatever it is."

"I don't think you can."

"Tell me." His fingers tightened on her arms.

"I can't go into this without you knowing the kind of woman I really am. What you're getting yourself into." She opened her eyes. "Did Keith tell you about his last conversation with me?"

His forehead creased, and he started to shake his head, then stopped. "About your ultimatum?"

"Right. So why are you talking of love? With *me*?"

"Because I love you." He chuckled, but his expression said he thought she'd lost her mind. "Am I missing something here?"

"It doesn't matter to you that I sent my husband to his grave thinking I didn't want to have any more children with him?"

His countenance stilled. "That was your ultimatum?"

"Yes."

"You don't want any more kids? Ever?" He was withdrawing from her. She could sense it. Pulling away emotionally even though he still held her to him.

"No. Yes. I mean I told him if he didn't resign from the army, come home, I didn't want any more children. I couldn't take it anymore, Bryce. Him being gone all the time, in constant danger. Me alone in Canyon Springs with Gina. It was foolish and childish, and I've regretted those words every day of my life."

"He never told me what you said, Sandi."

"But you just said you knew about my ultimatum."

"He didn't confide specifics."

She swallowed. "Then it must have wounded him deeply."

"I don't think so." He shook his head. "I saw Keith before he climbed on that copter for the last time. He didn't tell me the nature of your call. But he was in high spirits, plotting and planning how he'd woo you and win you over to his point of view."

She stared, not comprehending.

"In fact, his last words to me were 'wise up, buddy.

You need to get yourself right with God—and get yourself a woman like Sandi to boss you around. You're missing out on the fun of persuading her to change her mind.'"

"He said that?"

"I thought he was nuts, but he could hardly wait to get back to you and Gina—and start that persuasion." Bryce's eyes grew tender as he cupped her face in his two hands. "But you've lived the past five years carrying that burden, haven't you? Reliving your last words."

She nodded.

"What were his last words to *you,* Sandi?"

"He said—" Tears pricked as her mind unwillingly went back to that day. Again heard the sharpness in her voice. The anger. The selfishness. The wounding, hateful words.

She took a shaky breath, trying to remember Keith's response. His final words. "He said…he said, 'I love you.'"

With a gasp, her gaze sought that of Bryce. *Why had she never remembered that before?*

"See? He loved you." Bryce's hands tightened on her, his gaze gently insistent. "I'll never hope to replace Keith—but I love you, too."

He loved her. Bryce loved her.

"I don't deserve to be loved. By either of you."

"Nobody *deserves* to be loved, Sandi. That's what love is all about." He chuckled, his warm brown eyes twinkling. "So what would you say if I invited you and that little checklist of yours to boss me around— let's say, for a lifetime?"

Epilogue

Oh, man. Just his luck.

Sandi Bradshaw-soon-to-be-Harding.

His fiancée.

And Meg. They weren't supposed to be back from that Phoenix overnight shopping trip until Saturday evening. Not morning.

Bryce clapped a hand over Gina's mouth, swept her into his arms and ducked behind a U-Haul trailer parked outside the provisional museum at a Canyon Springs shopping plaza.

Wouldn't you know it. There went the surprise.

He had half a dozen historical society members painting walls. Kara, Devon—and LeAnne—cleaning storefront windows and miniblinds. Grandma Mae serving refreshments. And he, Trey and Joe still had to unpack a display case delivered late yesterday afternoon, then make dozens of trailer trips between the old and new facility. With the funding coming through for the firefighting job, there wasn't much time to get everything taken care of before he launched into exams and the training academy.

Car doors slammed. Familiar female laughter echoed across the parking lot.

"You can come out from your hidey-hole, Bryce," Meg called between giggles. "Sandi saw you. And it's a little hard to camouflage a dozen recognizable vehicles and that big trailer."

Sheepish, he stepped from behind the U-Haul and set Gina on her feet. Waving her U.S. Army cap, she charged toward her still-laughing mother and he followed along behind.

"Mommy! Mommy! What are you doing here? This is a surprise."

Sandi knelt for a hug, then stood to level a what-am-I-going-to-do-with-you look on him. But her eyes danced with the same love he knew reflected in his own.

"So what happened?" He slipped an arm around her waist, but turned an accusing glare on Meg. "Who's responsible for this breach of security? I want names. Ranks. Serial numbers."

Meg and Sandi pointed at each other.

"Oh? A collaboration, is it?"

Gina grabbed his free hand. "What's *laboration,* Uncle Bryce?"

"Collaboration in this instance means willingly assisting the enemy."

Sandi playfully punched him in the arm. "Since when am I the enemy?"

Meg laughed. "I can't be accused of aiding and abetting. More like breaking down under duress of intense cross-examination. Interrogation just short of bamboo shoots under the fingernails."

He pulled back from Sandi. "I knew you had some bossy inclinations, but nobody warned me about out-right torture. I might need to rethink this engagement stuff."

Grabbing a fistful of his shirt, her gaze flickered from his eyes to his mouth and back again. "Just try it, Sergeant, and you may find yourself begging for mercy."

"Sounds intriguing."

Gina tugged on his hand. "Mommy says you're going to be my new daddy?"

It was a question rather than a statement, as if seeking confirmation. He glanced at Sandi. So she'd talked to Gina about this. He'd never want the little girl to think he could replace Keith. Nobody, even on his best day, could ever replace his good buddy. Ever be a better dad than Keith would have been.

But he himself would be the only father Gina would remember. And he never wanted her to regret it. Sandi smiled encouragement, and he crouched down by the little girl. Tugged on the bill of her army cap. Looked her in the eye.

"I'd be proud to be your daddy—if you want me to be."

Gina studied him a long moment, her brow crinkled in concentration. Then her face brightened.

"Uncle Daddy!"

She flung her arms around his neck, all but squeezing the stuffin' out of him. He lifted her into his arms, then turned to the woman he loved. "Uncle Daddy, huh? I think we'll have to work on that one."

"I don't know." She tilted her head. "Has a nice ring to it, don't you think?"

"Guess it does at that. Kind of like our new place will. Hardings' Hideaway."

"I love that name."

"Grandma promises there will be frequent off-base outings to the park for a certain little someone when I'm not out on firefighting business. You know, to ensure coast-is-clear canoodling time."

"Ooooh. I like the sounds of that even better."

"Me, too." He gave the "certain little someone" snuggled in his arms a hug, then set her on the ground to race after Meg to the new facility.

"I guess you want a peek at the interim Canyon Springs Historical Museum?" He gave Sandi an admonishing look. "Admit it. You're back in town before you're supposed to be because you didn't think we could do it without you here to manage things. To boss us around."

"Speaking of which—" She rummaged in her purse. Pulled out a too-familiar red spiral notebook.

He groaned and tried to snatch it out of her hand, but with a laugh she spun away. Turned her back on him to run a finger down a tightly scripted page.

"It's not that bad." She gave him a flirty over-the-shoulder smile.

He narrowed his eyes. "I'll be the judge of that."

"Hmm. Let's see." She made a soft clucking sound with her tongue. "Oh, here's one you may like."

She snapped the notebook shut and sashayed back to his side, a smile playing on her lips.

"I don't think I want to hear it."

"Oh, but I think you do."

He heaved a beleaguered sigh. What did she have in mind for him this time? "Okay, let's have it."

Eyes dancing, she slipped her arms around his neck. Snuggled in close.

"What's this?" he pretended to protest, but slipped his hands around her waist. "Buttering me up for my chores?"

"Nooo." She placed a silencing finger to his lips.

"Spill it, soldier, or I'll throw you in the stockade."

She took a deep breath, eyes focused on his. "As happy as I am to now have the support of the society members, to feel at home in Canyon Springs at long last, the thing that makes me happiest is—"

"Yes?"

"Finding a home in *your* heart."

Man, that sounded good. His words came husky. "But about that chore you're withholding…"

She pulled slightly back in his arms. "Not to be diverted, are you?"

He shook his head.

She sighed, and behind his neck he could hear the

pages of the little notebook she still held flipping through her fingers. "Ah. Here it is."

He groaned in resignation.

"Page fifteen. Line three."

Get ready. Here it comes.

Then he heard the notebook drop to the ground behind him.

And slowly, tantalizingly, her sweet mouth smiled up at him, sparkling eyes gazing deeply into his. Man, she was buttering him up. Big-time. Must be a chore to end all chores.

"So, here it is, Sergeant," came her breathless whisper. "Kiss your fiancée—and that's an order."

Heart soaring, he responded with a hearty laugh.

Would have saluted, too, but he found himself otherwise engaged.

* * * * *

Dear Reader,

I hope you've enjoyed your return visit to mountain country, Canyon Springs, Arizona! There's nothing more magical than a high-country summer day, with the scent of sun-warmed or rain-washed ponderosa pine permeating the air, bluer than blue skies and evenings so cool you'd better bring a jacket!

I have to admit that when I was "introduced" to heroine Sandi Bradshaw and her deceased husband's best friend, Bryce Harding, I wondered how on earth these two lonely, stubborn people could ever find a happily-ever-after with each other.

But Matthew 19:26 says "With God all things are possible." Which is something we need to keep in mind when situations and challenges in our own lives appear daunting and dreams far away. Does that verse mean we'll always get our own way, that we'll get everything in life we want? No, but it does mean that if we put our trust in God, He will be right there to forgive, encourage, comfort and give us the strength to get through whatever we may face.

This past year has been a special one for me—liberally peppered with encouraging reader letters (thank you!) and the news that my very first book, *Dreaming of Home,* won several prestigious contests!

I hope *At Home in His Heart* touched *your* heart. I love to hear from readers, so please contact me via email at glynna@glynnakaye.com or c/o Love

Inspired Books, 233 Broadway, Suite 1001, New York, NY 10279. Please also visit my website at www.glynnakaye.com—and stop in at www.seekerville.blogspot.com and www.loveinspiredauthors.com to meet and greet my writer friends!

Glynna Kaye

Questions for Discussion

1. Bryce Harding tried to talk his buddy out of marrying Sandi Bradshaw. How did his background and his relationships with his mother and LeAnne color his thoughts and determination?

2. Since her husband's death, Sandi has allowed her mother-in-law to become more involved in her life than is healthy for either of them. Can you understand how that might happen? Why is it so important to Sandi to win her mother-in-law's favor? Have you ever allowed yourself to become more focused on pleasing a person than pleasing God?

3. For years Sandi secretly regretted her last words to her husband. Why do you think it is so hard for her to accept God's forgiveness? Have you ever said or done something that you've been unwilling to forgive yourself for, even though the Bible clearly states that if you ask Him for forgiveness, you *are* forgiven?

4. When his best buddy died, Bryce determined he didn't want to live the rest of his life with regrets. So why does he feel guilty when he begins to take serious notice of Sandi?

5. Gina takes a shine to "Uncle Bryce" at their first meeting, much to Sandi's chagrin. What is it about

him that Gina quickly recognizes but that Sandi is unwilling to acknowledge? How can a child sometimes see clearly things that an adult cannot?

6. Bryce refers to himself as New Bryce and Old Bryce. Why do you think he feels vulnerable at the thought of joining a Bible study? How might he benefit from meeting with other men?

7. Sandi says she has no intention of remarrying—and she's serious. What is it about Bryce that causes her to reconsider opening her heart? How is he different from her husband? How are they alike?

8. Bryce is devastated when he realizes his earlier perceptions of Sandi were based on erroneous assumptions. Have you ever made negative assumptions about someone and later had your eyes opened to the truth that you judged them wrongly? How did that affect you? What actions did you take—or do you still need to take?

9. Sandi keeps herself busy—seldom allowing time for reflection or doing anything special for herself. How does that help her cope with being a widow and single mom? How has it harmed her?

10. Because of his background, Bryce struggles with the concept of mutual submission in marriage. Where do you see evidence that he begins to un-

derstand the true intention of God's plan? That it's not about who's the boss, but about caring more for someone else than you do yourself?

11. Sandi recognizes her earlier immaturity in the way she treated her husband. How did her fear for his safety, her loneliness and having a sick child push her to react the way she did? Her husband loved her, but how might he have better helped her deal with his absence? How might a stronger relationship with God have helped her cope?

12. Due to the hoopla accompanying the newspaper photo, an uncertainty with their budding relationship quickly develops between Sandi and Bryce. Both are hurt but feel they're doing the other a favor by backing off. What in their backgrounds contributed to this abrupt decision? How might they have better communicated?

13. Bryce tells Sandi she's given the museum and the dreamed-of veterans exhibit first place in her life. Do you agree—or not? Why is it so hard for her to set aside the past so she can move into the future? Do you believe in the coming years that Sandi's involvement in the museum will be a healthier one? Why or why not?

14. Sandi comes to realize that LeAnne's opposition to Bryce has more to do with LeAnne's own in-

securities and loneliness than it does with Bryce himself. How might Sandi help her mother-in-law and herself transition to a healthier, more balanced relationship?

15. Given their backgrounds, experiences and beliefs about themselves, what challenges do you think Sandi and Bryce will encounter in the future as they grow and mature in their life together?

LARGER-PRINT BOOKS!

GET 2 FREE LARGER-PRINT NOVELS PLUS 2 FREE MYSTERY GIFTS

Love Inspired ®
SUSPENSE
RIVETING INSPIRATIONAL ROMANCE

Larger-print novels are now available...

LARGER-PRINT BOOKS!

**GET 2 FREE
LARGER-PRINT NOVELS
PLUS 2 FREE
MYSTERY GIFTS**

Love Inspired®

Larger-print novels are now available...

LILP11B